MW01516451

NORTH POLE UNLIMITED COLLECTION 1

DECKER AND JOY, HOLLIS AND IVY

ELLE RUSH

SBD ENTERTAINMENT

DECKER AND JOY

A North Pole Unlimited Romance
By
Elle Rush

BLURB

He was looking for an A.W.O.L. elf, not a date with the kitten foster-mom who was one of his suspects.

Somebody messed up and let a prototype escape from North Pole Unlimited's top secret Toys and Research Division. Now P.I. Decker Harkness has the contract to track it down. He's not exactly sure what E.L.V.I.S does, but he's hot on the trail.

Joy McCall has her hands full of foster animals and pet treats at Kitten Caboodle, but she's not too busy to notice strange goings-on at the pet shelter where she works.

When their paths cross during a triple kitten-napping, Decker and Joy will have to work together to close their cases. Will everyone make it home to celebrate a merry Christmas together?

Only Santa knows.

PROLOGUE

MID-OCTOBER

North Pole Unlimited Headquarters,
December, Manitoba, Canada (25 kilometres south-east of Winnipeg)

Nick Klassen, soon-to-be the new vice-president of Human Resources at North Pole Unlimited, knocked on the C.E.O.'s door with his free hand. "Hi, Gran. Jilly said you wanted to see me?"

The woman behind the massive oak desk was an impressive seventy-five. Her steel grey hair didn't dare escape from the bun on the back of her head, but her face was all smiles. "Nick, come in. Pull up a chair and let's chat," the company president said.

The meeting request had come out of nowhere, and Nick wasn't certain of the reason. He was preparing to take over for the retiring VP, and had a lot left to learn. He wouldn't be surprised if she were checking on him to ensure the handover was going well.

"How's my favorite grandson's love life?"

Boss or not, he wasn't answering that. He decided to misdirect. "I'm your favorite?"

"For the purpose of this meeting you are. Are you seeing anybody these days?"

He choked on his coffee. "Not at the moment. My hands are too full taking over the reins from George to have a social life." North Pole Unlimited had thousands of employees around the world. With their strict employment contracts, Nick would be responsible for each and every one. He didn't need any distractions while he learned to keep track of everybody in all the different divisions in all the different countries where the company operated.

"You know a balanced life is important for all NPU employees. There's a lovely young woman in—"

"No, Gran!" He was not being set up by his grandmother.

"Fine, fine." She waved her hand at him, and Nick saw a faint tremor. He was glad she'd be stepping down in the new year. Adelaide Klassen always said she loved her work, but she deserved a retirement while she was healthy enough to enjoy it. "Let's get down to business then."

"Yes, let's." Before she pulled out her phone to show him a picture of the lovely young woman, since Nick knew she'd have one.

She picked away at her keyboard and displayed her email on the large screen which hung over the fireplace mantle in the corner of her office. "Dr. Farnsworth is still looking for a new assistant. She wants someone before Christmas. How is that coming?"

"We have a bunch of promising applicants we're working through," Nick replied.

"Work quickly. Also, I want you to check with Andrea personally. She might already have somebody in mind."

Which meant she did. Nick worked the same way. "Speaking of somebody in mind, I wanted to talk to you about a potential new security chief." He pointed at an unopened email on the screen. "The one marked Decker Harkness."

His grandmother opened it and clicked on the attachment. A photo of a stern, brush-cut man in his late thirties popped up. "He looks like a cop," she said.

"He was with the Ottawa Police Service for fifteen years before he left with a work-related injury. Now he's a private detective in the area. We've used him before. He's competent, quick and discreet."

She clicked on the next photo, showing a younger, equally serious Decker in his police uniform. "Does he ever smile?"

"Not that I've noticed." Decker was good at his job, but they hadn't had much social interaction. Nick had hired him to do background checks on potential employees, hunt down owners of properties that NPU and their affiliates wanted to acquire, and investigate claims made against the company. Every report he'd received had exceeded expectations.

Decker Harkness was exactly the type of security professional North Pole Unlimited needed. He had practical experience in the field, and had done a supervisory stint in the Computer Forensics unit while he was recovering from his injury. In addition to NPU's physical security concerns, the attacks on the company's servers were increasing again with the announcement of this year's new computer game which was coming out for the holidays. The little hacker punks couldn't access their air-gapped systems for the cheat codes, but they didn't know that. It was a problem Nick couldn't afford to ignore. They needed Decker, or someone else, to oversee it all. With the current security chief following George out the door, NPU had to hire somebody sooner rather than later.

He shook his head as he thought of something else.

"What is it?" she asked.

"I just realized we are going to be having a huge turnover on the board over the next couple years." Some replacements were already lined up, but finding the others would all fall to him.

"Then I suggest you start filling them as soon as possible. Does Mr. Harkness know what we do here?"

"Not exactly. He's been receiving standard freelance assignments from us."

His grandmother clucked through closed teeth. "That's not good, Nick." She closed her email and clicked a file on her desktop marked "Top Secret".

Nick recognized the project specs which appeared on the screen. "What about it?" The prototype was still in its testing phase in the Research and Development department. It was going to be huge once it got to market, but at the moment, there were a few...bugs.

"Tinka—Dr. Kovac—was running some trials out of the lab."

"And?" he asked. Because there had to be an "and" with a set-up that good.

"And it might have gotten away from her."

"Might have?"

"She's still searching the area. There's a slim chance it

made it onto a truck. With a shipment headed to Ottawa," his grandmother continued.

He looked around for the nearest flat surface to bang his head against. Malfunctioning proprietary technology on the loose? That was a disaster waiting to happen. Nick eyed her desk. It looked sturdy enough to knock him out of his misery.

"We'll give her a couple days to find it. Think of it this way," she said with another smile. "If she can't, it will be an excellent test. If Mr. Harkness can solve our little problem, you know he'll be perfect for the job."

1. DECKER

LATE OCTOBER
Ottawa, Ontario

A year after hanging out his shingle as a private investigator, his dream of being a private detective was dying a painful death. Decker Harkness needed an income-generating, career-making case if he wanted to keep the doors open, and he needed it yesterday. Strip-mall office rent was all he could afford, but he wouldn't even be able to manage that if things didn't pick up soon.

He didn't mind doing corporate security checks. They could be boring, but he was good at online investigations. Second best were the fraud cases his insurance-agent friends occasionally tossed his way. He was tired of the divorce and custody cases which paid most of his bills. They were beginning to permanently tarnish his view of humanity.

Which was why the email from North Pole Unlimited came at the perfect time. Decker had done a handful of jobs for NPU in the last year—employment checks on locals, tracking down owners of property they wanted to buy—but the message he received the day before hinted at a much bigger case. Proprietary technological information and potential corporate espionage were mentioned and set his heart racing. Decker had waited months for this kind of opportunity.

He pulled out one of his surviving suit jackets from his Ottawa Police Service days, and pressed his shirt and tie. He took a moment to check his fresh buzz cut in the mirror, and was pleased with how it hid the half-dozen silver hairs invading the brown at his temples. He looked ready to deal with a sensitive, classified problem for an international, multi-million-dollar company.

He'd even cleaned his office, sort of. He scanned the room one more time. His university diploma was visible on the wall behind him, as was his graduation picture from the police academy, and the photo of him getting his ten-year pin from the mayor. His office wasn't big, but he only did the parts the camera would catch.

It all looked good, except for the bald, lumbering black man who appeared outside his office door window holding two coffee cups. "Harkness, what are you doing in there? Open up!"

"Charlie? What's wrong?"

Charlie Barr had been his partner, first on patrol and later again when they'd worked together in Robbery. They'd kept in touch after Decker had left the force, but their run-ins had grown fewer and further between as their jobs pulled them in separate directions.

Decker unlocked the door and relieved Charlie of one of his cups before he cleared the threshold. "This is a surprise."

"But a surprise with coffee," Charlie said, his rough smoker's voice mangling the words.

"Which means you want something." He didn't mind.

"A sounding board. A new shoplifting ring has popped up with one of my sergeants. Get this. They use coupons," Charlie said.

"If they have coupons, it's not shoplifting."

"If they have legitimate coupons, it's not. This crew is printing and distributing them. Then, when the store is swamped with people wanting their freebies, they take their pick of the merchandise and walk out the door in all the confusion."

Why couldn't he have had this kind of case while he was still on the force? It was more challenging to catch thieves who used their brains instead of their brawn. Then he had a sip of the coffee Charlie had brought him, and remembered a perk of being self-employed: no more squad-room java. "That's incredibly low tech. Aren't they worried about security cameras?" Decker asked.

"When I say swamping the store, I mean close to a hundred shoppers descending at once. They target small stores where crowding is an issue."

"How can I help?" Charlie had shown up for some unofficial assistance, whether he admitted it or not. His old partner was a great cop, with an infallible ability to sniff out evidence, but his memory was horrible. Charlie had bought three copies of the same memory improvement book in the time they worked together, and he'd read them all.

"What was the name of the printer from that art gallery case we worked a few years ago? The one making the prints but wasn't legally complicit because they thought they had a contract? When was that?"

"Three years ago. Rainbow Ink. Wasn't it in your file notes?" As Charlie had said, the case had gone nowhere; no wonder he didn't recall the details.

"I didn't remember where I put them, and you were closer," Charlie said. "A cup of coffee is cheaper than asking the file clerk to pull everything."

Decker's computer beeped to signal the start of his video conference.

"I'll get out of your hair since you obviously have a date," Charlie teased.

"It's a business meeting. And at least I have hair," Decker countered.

"Well, if you're going to insult me, I'll leave." Charlie laughed on his way out. "Thanks for the help," he yelled as the door clicked shut.

When Decker answered the video call, he was surprised to see Nick Klassen at the other end of it. All his prior contracts with North Pole Unlimited originated with George Macintyre. When Nick explained that he was stepping in as the new vice-president of human resources, Decker offered his congratulations. "That's great. Please tell George to enjoy his retirement and go after all those fish he was talking about. I'm pleased that you thought of me. I hope we can continue working together."

His new employer nodded in agreement. "Me, too. This call wasn't just to inform you about George's retire-ment. As I mentioned in my email yesterday, I have a deli-cate situation that I need your help with."

Decker leaned closer to the screen, one hand gripping the pen he used to take notes. Nick might know who he was, but that didn't mean anything. Decker needed to prove himself all over again. He was up to the task;

impressing a new—sort of new—client could lead to lots of work, and he needed every bit he could get if he wanted his business to stay afloat. There was no case too big or small for Harkness investigations.

Although this one was definitely on the small side. "You want me to find a doll?" Decker repeated for the third time. "An E.L.V.I.S. doll?" His alarm bells were clanging; the case couldn't be as easy as Nick was presenting it as.

"It's a prototype," Nick explained. "A very expensive one. It has some animatronic components and some recording playback devices that aren't ready for consumer use, which is why we need it back. We've been working on this project for years as a replacement for an existing product. E.L.V.I.S. accidentally went to a store in your area which sells our Funster pet toy line. Unfortunately, we aren't certain which location it was shipped to. I'm going to send you a list. We need you to visit the stores, find it, and retrieve it at any cost. The unit has a GPS chip installed. That should help you."

"Why can't you track it with the GPS?" Decker asked. He wanted the business, but this was basically running an errand. It wasn't the stepping stone to bigger, more important cases he'd hoped for from NPU. If anything, it was a demotion. But if the situation were as insignificant as it seemed, why would a vice-president be involved? Something was fishy about the entire setup.

"The chip is currently on the fritz. It broadcasts, but only on an extremely limited range. That's one of the kinks we need to work out. E.L.V.I.S. can't be running around in the wild, Decker. I cannot emphasize how important it is to get it back to our labs as soon as possible. Can you handle this?" The blond giant leaned into the lens on his computer. "You'll have a week to find E.L.V.I.S. We can't give you any longer."

A week to recover a doll? Now Decker was insulted, but he didn't let it show. "No problem," he assured the man on the screen. The job wasn't what he'd thought it would be, but it was one less cheating spouse he'd have to follow. And recovering private property was a legitimate job.

"Excellent. We've sent an encrypted email to your account. My assistant Jilly will text you the security password. We'll include a picture and some of the specs for you. There will also be a link to the GPS tracker and a list of the stores where it might have been sent. I'll expect daily progress reports, Decker. Again, I cannot emphasize how dangerous this can be in the wrong hands. Good luck." The screen went dead.

It was a doll. How much trouble could it be?

The email arrived in his inbox moments after he shut down the video link. Decker spent the rest of the morning studying the file. The prototype looked like G.I. Joe and Malibu Ken had a secret love child. The figure in the photo had a black, plastic pompadour and a shiny utility belt over its navy ninja suit. Decker didn't have children, but he didn't see it appealing to boys or to girls. Then again, he didn't have to play with it. He just had to find it.

The GPS app which Nick's assistant sent was simple to use. Unfortunately, the results were inconclusive. It displayed a large circle around Archer Plaza, a two-story shopping center off the Queensway, before flashing an error message and dying. Decker couldn't tell if the problem was with the app or E.L.V.I.S. Three of the possible locations on Decker's list were in that area. It was convenient for narrowing his search, but it meant he had to brave a mall. A week before Halloween. And the night before, he'd seen a news segment about how some stores were already putting up Christmas decorations. E.L.V.I.S.'s timing was terrible.

He started the search as soon as the mall opened the next morning. Nothing impressed clients like fast results.

His first stop was equally inoffensive and unmemorable. Fins and Things was a small store specializing in terrariums and aquariums, and in the fish, lizards, and snakes to fill them. It only had a small bin of toys for other animals. Their biweekly supply order arrived while Decker was in the store, and when they checked the box in front of him, they came up empty. They were definitely off his list.

He hesitated outside Kitten Caboodle, another store on the mall's main level. Decker peered through the window and was impressed with what he saw. A private animal shelter and adoption center took up half the space; the rest was a fully stocked pet store. This was a place pets and owners would appreciate. Bright, clean, well laid out. He spotted a full aisle of toys running the length of the store, and that didn't include the stuffed animals tucked among the other merchandise.

Kitten Caboodle was a contender.

2. JOY

"OH, THANK YOU, DELIVERY FAIRIES!" Joy McCall clapped her hands together at the sight of the man wheeling a trolley through the front doors of Kitten Caboodle. She refrained from jumping in deference to the orange kitten on her shoulder. Its little claws were dug in tightly to her navy knit cardigan, but the little thing wasn't strong enough to withstand that level of shaking.

Joy plucked the cat from her top and set it in the glass-sided display box which acted like a playpen. "In you go, Pumpkin." The kitten toddled toward the pile of napping fluff balls in the corner. He immediately snuggled with the three nearly identical black brothers who were even tinier than he was. Spooky, Midnight, and Stinky Spice, like Pumpkin, had two speeds: espresso high and asleep. Joy was grateful for the temporary break. It had been kitten-palooza lately.

A pair of teenagers had found Pumpkin near an apartment complex by the mall. Joy offered to hand-feed him until he was fully weaned. A few days later, a pregnant black cat had been left in a box at the shelter's back door. The poor thing had been in bad shape but still managed to deliver three healthy kittens before she passed away, and Joy volunteered for more foster kitten duty.

It was a twenty-four-hour-a-day job, and had taken a month, but Joy and the cats had survived all the late-night feedings. Fortunately, working in a shelter meant Joy could keep them in the store during her shifts and bundle them up in a carrier for the trips back and forth to her apartment.

After making sure the kittens were settled for the moment, Joy helped unload the boxes full of goodies. Once she signed for them, she was left with four cases of the newest Funsters from North Pole Unlimited's online catalogue. "Okay, listen up," she said. The store was empty except for the animals in it. "These toys are for paying customers. No knocking them off shelves. No chewing on the packaging. No playing with them. Paws off."

Mitzi, the miniature schnauzer Kitten Caboodle had temporarily taken in while her owner was hospitalized, lifted her head from her doggie bed and yawned in Joy's direction. "Excellent. Good job paying attention, every-body. I should have prefaced that with T-R-E..." All heads in the shop were turned in her direction by the second letter of the word treats. "That's all I am to you, isn't it? Your personal chef. Fine. I'll remember this," Joy muttered as she began pulling the boxes behind the counter. "You'd miss me if I left."

The store went silent, and Joy wished she could take it back. But it was true. After years of applying for local veterinary assistant positions, she'd taken the plunge and registered with an employment agency. They hadn't got back to her yet, but Joy was ever-hopeful that she would find a job in the area.

Something that would give her a bump in pay so she could get a bigger place. Maybe even a house someday. Until a few weeks ago, she hadn't considered the possibility of owning cats, not where she was currently living. It was next to impossible to find an apartment that would take one pet, let alone four. She needed to find her boys forever homes, but for the moment, Joy was burying her head in the sand.

She wouldn't give up the ungrateful beasts to just anyone, which was why Kitten Caboodle ran background checks on their customers before they left the shelter with an animal. Every soul in the store went home with an award-winning human. Joy couldn't keep all their rescue animals, no matter how much she wanted to, so she did her best to make sure they got the best of everything.

That included toys, and NPU products were top notch. The company's stuffed animals were tear-resistant, and their iron-hide chew toys lasted forever. "Oh, you guys should see the new stuff," she told them. Joy quickly sorted and shelved the contents of the first two crates, taking a moment to cuddle the fluffy lions and tigers. Another indicator of NPU's quality was that they didn't mess around when they shipped things. There was a hole torn in the bottom of the third container, but it looked to have been resealed with packing tape. None the contents listed on the invoice were missing. North Pole Unlimited was a quality outfit all the way around.

Joy was transferring the last of the catnip-stuffed mice into the bin with the latching, pet-proof lid when the dark-haired man who had been staring through the window for the last five minutes finally made his move.

He was cute. Clean-cut. Well-dressed for a casual outfit. His khakis and forest green shirt were nearly new. He didn't have a jacket, but he didn't need one for the unseasonably mild late-October weather. Joy didn't realize how tall he was until he got closer. Her eyes were level with the dimple he had at the side of his mouth. "Hi," she said.

He stared at her for a second and squinted at the nametag on her chest. "Hello, Joy. I'm Decker."

"Hi, Decker. Can I help you today?"

"I truly hope so. Do you have any Funsters? It's a line of pet toys."

It was an odd request; customers never asked for toys by brand. "Absolutely. Almost a whole aisle full, in fact. Are you looking for anything in particular? Who for? Cat? Small dog? Big dog?" He looked like the big dog type. Not a Rottweiler or pit bull. Maybe a husky.

"I'm looking for a doll. About this big." He held his hands a foot apart. "It has dark clothes and it moves. Kind of like an army action figure."

"I didn't know Funsters came as dolls. I can tell you we don't have any." Human-shaped animal toys were never a big seller.

He shook his head insistently. "I happen to know NPU accidentally sent one to a store in the area. Kitten Caboodle was on their list. I really need to find that doll. Can you please double-check your stock?" Decker asked. He took off his Senators cap, as if it would make him appear more earnest.

It worked. The poor fellow looked as disappointed as he sounded. At the rate he was wringing his cap brim, it was going to be a perfect circle by the end of the day. "I think there might be a little left to sort through in this last box," she relented.

Decker leaned over her shoulder as she emptied the last carton. He smelled like—she inhaled again—sugar cookies. An unusual scent for a man, but it worked for him.

"Lions and tigers and bears. Nothing else," she said. "Sorry, no doll. I can keep my eyes open if you'd like."

His frown didn't last long, but Joy knew she saw it. "That's okay. Thanks for looking. Maybe I'll check out your store for a bit," he said.

"Let me know if you need help."

She kept an eye on him as he perused everything. *Everything.* He didn't seem to have a preference for either cat or dog items. And the man was not afraid to get dirty. Although he had to be six feet tall, he went up on his toes to search the back of the top shelves. Then he knelt to see everything she had on the floor, which was bags of dog food and kitty litter.

"Are you looking for anything in particular? Aside from the doll?" Joy asked as he moved to the last row.

"No."

As he bent to check the bottom shelf, Joy noticed Pumpkin had abandoned his nap in favor of the new plaything in front of him. She wasn't sure how the cat had managed to get up to the top of the playpen's glass wall, but the kitten was wobbling on the narrow wooden edge.

Then he launched.

Pumpkin's little legs splayed out. The fur ball didn't get much lift or distance from his pathetic jump. He just fell. Luckily for him, Decker's back made the drop only a foot.

Unluckily for Decker, the fleece he was wearing looked thicker than it apparently was.

"Yeow!"

Joy wasn't sure if the scream came from the man or the cat.

3. DECKER

IS that what a bed of nails felt like? Decker had been examining the store's merchandise, looking to see if E.L.V.I.S. was misplaced behind any of the massive bags of dog food, when an unknown assailant jammed a dozen knives into his back. He was ex-police and a private detective; nobody should have gotten the drop on him. He'd scanned the store when he entered. He was the only person in it, aside from Joy. She was unnervingly pretty with her auburn hair and brown eyes, but she hadn't registered as a cold-blooded killer.

The razors trying to sever his spine moved. Decker tensed his thighs, preparing to spring backward and crush the attacker against one of the metal shelving racks, when a warm hand fell on the back of his neck. He stilled instantly.

"Don't move," Joy whispered.

Decker felt a slight pressure, and then the needles were extracted from his skin, one by one. He slowly stood and wondered if he'd get to the emergency room before he bled to death. One of the blades may have hit an artery.

"Are you okay, sweetie?" Joy asked.

"I'm not sure." He wasn't light-headed, and he was moving okay. There was surprisingly little pain. He might make it.

"I was talking to the cat."

Cat? Decker turned and found Joy cuddling an orange kitten as she examined its feet. "Pumpkin, what were you thinking? You could have been hurt jumping like that." The beast in her arms *meeped*. "Okay, you look fine. No more pouncing on innocent customers, Pumpkin. Say you're sorry."

The kitten yawned at him.

"Your cat almost mauled me to death," Decker said. Cats were vicious, which was why he didn't have one. Give him a friendly, loyal mutt any day. "You should have it declawed."

Joy gently hooked one of the kitten's paws and lifted it. "Pumpkin isn't a thing. He's a baby. He has baby claws. See?"

No, he couldn't. Decker couldn't see any kind of claw at all. He reached for the offered paw and ran his finger over the pad. Finally, a glimpse of white nail poked the fleshy part of his fingertip before it disappeared again. How had something so tiny caused so much agony?

"Again, I'm sorry. He's usually such a sweetie. Unlike the terrible trio," Joy said.

"Terrible trio?"

She cuddled the little cat in her arms and nodded toward the glass case behind him where three black kittens were stretching. They looked utterly harmless. Decker reached into the bin to pet them.

"Do they have names?"

"I call them the Spice Boys. Midnight, Spooky, and Stinky."

"With big brother Pumpkin Spice?" Decker asked.

Joy smiled and shrugged.

"Spooky and Midnight I get, but why Stinky?"

The little guy rolled over to allow Decker to rub his belly, then let out an eye-watering fart a saber-toothed tiger would have been proud of. "Never mind," he said.

"Are you okay?" Joy asked.

Decker didn't have time to process the soft tone in Joy's words or the spark that flared when she touched his hand because the heat-seeking missile in her arms jumped at him again.

This time the kitten used its claws to scramble up his shirt until it perched on his shoulder. A tickle under his chin built, then disappeared, as the short tail fanned back and forth across his face. "*Meep meep*," the kitten chirped before it stuck its nose in Decker's neck. Two tiny little legs wrapped themselves around his throat. It was a hug.

He wasn't completely heartless. The little fuzz ball was obviously sorry. "Okay, Punk, enough."

The cat *meeped* one more time, then let go and balanced on his shoulder. Decker held perfectly still while Joy lifted the cat off him and replaced it in the glass case. He caught a whiff of something floral and green when a lock of Joy's hair came untucked from behind her ear and brushed his nose. She was really very pretty. Not that he hadn't had a chance to notice before, but now she was too close to ignore.

Pretty, kind, funny. It was the ideal cover for somebody who'd steal something from a shipment. Nobody was as perfect as Joy looked.

"Did you find it?" she asked.

"Find what?"

"Whatever you were looking for on the bottom shelf before Pumpkin decided to say hello."

"I thought somebody else might have put the doll out on a shelf without you knowing about it. Can I leave my number in case you come across the Funster I'm looking for?" He pulled out one of his business cards. Joy slipped it into her shirt pocket, promising to keep an eye out for it. Then he left to hit the final stop on his list.

He found Pure Brewed & Pure Bred on the second floor at the far end of the mall. It was a pet-friendly coffee shop attached to what the sign called a "non-human boutique." Decker stopped before he crossed the threshold. He'd heard about places like this, but he'd never been forced to enter one before. If he were a dog that had to wear one of the overpriced sweaters he saw in the store's window, he'd pull a Cujo before his owners knew what was happening. He entered through the coffee shop, figuring he'd ease into his investigation.

The barista gave him a severe once-over before frowning and waving him to the counter. "What can I get you? Drip coffee, black?"

He was going to choke on every mouthful, but it would be worth it. "No, a triple shot grande caramel macchiato with double whip and half and half, and sprinkles, but chocolate only, not the colored ones. Please." He'd rather have had the French roast drip, black, but he refused to give the judgmental coffee-slinger the satisfaction.

The barista's pierced eyebrow went up and she nodded slightly, as if he'd somewhat redeemed himself with his answer. "Anything else?"

He glanced at the thin slices of sugar-covered cake in

the pastry case but they didn't appeal to him. He shook his head, and she turned her back to him while she made his order.

Tiny dogs in sweaters. Cats in harnesses and leashes. Decker was pretty sure he saw a ferret in a purse. Those weren't pets. What was wrong with dogs? Real dogs. Give him a husky or a German shepherd any day, not something he'd kill if he didn't watch his step. He sipped and saw the barista staring at him expectantly. He pressed his lips together, like he was tasting something unsavory, and walked into the store. The "harrumph" he heard behind him made the sugary swill worth it.

More people, and animals dressed like people, clogged the aisles of Pure Bred. Decker slowly made his way through the store. He had no idea pet owners paid such outrageous amounts for such unnecessary accessories. Did they need to have both hemp and bamboo collar options? And the toys. Two rows of them. "Excuse me, do you have any Funsters?" Decker asked an employee who was restocking a swivel rack displaying birthday cards for birds.

He was met with a sneer. "Funsters? We don't like to stock a lesser quality brand like that, but we have to since they are so popular with low-end pet owners. They're in the next aisle over," the young man with the "Liam" name tag said.

"I'm looking for a special item. Unique. It won't have been listed on any shipping manifest."

Liam's eyes opened wide. "Oh. Oh! I'm sorry, sir, I didn't realize you were one of our *unique customers*."

Decker heard the emphasis, despite the fact the shelf stocker's voice dropped to a whisper on the last two words. What was a unique customer? Did Pure Bred have a secret underground Funster black market operating out of their store? Had other prototypes been sent here accidentally? Or, worse for NPU, on purpose? "Yes, I am a unique customer," Decker lied.

"We don't currently have any of the Bombay cats we advertised on our private boards, but our exclusive breeders promised we'll be receiving a shipment in the next week or so. Since you're here in person today, we can put you on the waiting list for our first kindle."

"I don't want an e-reader. I want a cat." Decker didn't want a cat either, but he did want access to the suspicious-sounding private boards. If E.L.V.I.S. had been sent to Pure Bred, that seemed like the place he'd find out about it.

"Exactly. We'll get you set up."

"For what?"

"The first kindle."

Rather than repeat himself, Decker leveled a stare that had made hardened suspects quiver.

His current nemesis teared up. "I wasn't talking about e-readers. A kindle is a group of kittens," Liam said.

"Technically, yes, but it's generally called a litter. Unless you want to sound pretentious. Who do I talk to about a Bombay?" Decker asked. He might not be a cop anymore, but something had his crime-sense tingling. The fact the college-aged retail worker still hadn't answered his question about whether or not E.L.V.I.S. had been shipped to the store hadn't gone unnoticed either.

Liam led him past the checkout counter to the manager's office in the back. "Miss Drummond, this customer is interested in a *unique item*," he told his boss.

"Two items," Decker corrected. "I'm looking for one particular Funster which may have been shipped to your store. A moveable figurine, twelve inches tall, dressed somewhere between a G.I. Joe and a Ken doll. I want it. Also, tell me about the cats."

The manager, Lorraine Drummond, was an anti-hipster. In fact, she so strongly reminded Decker of a stereotypical librarian, it almost took her back around to hipster again. Her hair was pulled into a severe bun, she wore a navy suit with the blouse buttoned all the way to the collar, and glasses hung around her neck on a thick gold chain. She was still years from her thirtieth birthday. The dichotomy was jarring. "I'm not sure what you mean," Lorraine stalled, badly.

"A cat. Specifically, a Bombay. Liam said you were getting some in soon."

"Liam was speaking out of turn. First, I'm certain we wouldn't have ordered a Funster doll, of all things. Their regular products are bad enough. We recommend our clients purchase quality toys for their fur babies. Secondly, we have no cats available for purchase."

Decker knew he could walk away; they didn't seem to have what he was looking for. With Pure Bred's attitude, they'd have been happy to sell E.L.V.I.S. to him to get rid of the item before the bourgeois stink infected their store. But their rude, contemptuous attitude, the fact he'd struck out looking for the prototype, and the itch between his shoulder blades when it came to the non-existent cats they may or may not be selling kept him in place. Even if it did mean pretending to be interested in a "fur baby." He laid a business card that only listed his name and number on Lorraine's desk, and tapped it with his finger. "I expect a call when the cats come in. Liam said by the end of the week. I'll see you soon."

Fins and Things had been a wash. As had Kitten Caboodle. Pure Bred wasn't looking good either.

For a piece-of-cake job, he'd gotten nowhere. Decker returned to his office and reviewed the file Nick Klassen had sent, thinking he'd missed something. He didn't get any calls, from Joy or from Lorraine, which left him plenty of time to research Bombay cats.

Just in case.

4. JOY

JOY NEEDED a brick to weigh down the lid she'd slapped over the kittens' temporary play box. The adorable little buggers had escaped three times. Pumpkin got out alone twice; the last time he'd led Spooky and Stinky in an attempted mass rebellion. As much as Joy loved them, she looked forward to the day they were fully capable of handling cat food and litter boxes on their own. She didn't begrudge them her time, but she was spread so thin she was see-through.

She returned to her paperwork. She really disliked the managerial part of her job. Kitten Caboodle's lease was coming up and the mall was stalling on the renewal. It wasn't a matter of business; it was about competition. Specifically, it was about Pure Bred and Pure Brewed. The pet store and coffee shop on the second floor wanted to expand into consignment purebred pet sales. The management company they both dealt with was turning the situation into the O.K. Corral, declaring the mall wasn't big enough for the two of them.

Joy hadn't gone to veterinary college to negotiate

rental contracts. She'd earned her degree to help animals. But she had to do the first to do the second. Spooky, Midnight, Stinky, and Pumpkin were straining the shelter's capacity, but they had a good thing going on. Joy wasn't going to let some soulless store selling dog sweaters drive them out.

The shelter wasn't going down without a fight. Since she couldn't take the Spice Boys herself, Joy intended to make sure they found the second-most perfect home she could find by proving Kitten Caboodle was the place to be. It certainly had been a few hours ago. Joy needed more people like Decker Harkness in the store. If she stood him in the window holding a kitten, the line to the cash register would be out the door.

Joy wished she had received the doll he was looking for. Maybe if they'd had more of a chance to talk, she'd have worked up the nerve to ask if he wanted to join her for a coffee.

A flurry of barking erupted behind her. "It's me! Down, Mitzi. You'd think I was a stranger breaking in to rob the joint," a masculine voice announced from the kennel room, which was attached to the play room. Rob Allan was a veterinarian and Kitten Caboodle's owner. He'd hired Joy two years earlier. He said she could play manager while he played with the animals. He got the better part of the deal.

"Rob, I'm leaving you for four younger men," Joy shouted back as she loaded her kittens into a carrier.

"Take off. I've got this."

She left knowing the rest of the animals were in good hands. Rob took the evening shift, caring for and feeding the four rescue dogs and seven full-grown cats they had in the shelter, reviewing the store's sales numbers, and keeping the animals company until about nine o'clock.

Then she'd return at eight to do it all over again.

The next morning, she took two steps into the store and knew it was going to be one of those days. Her boss was a decent guy, but he'd obviously been distracted the night before. Mitzi, or one of the store's other four-legged occupants, had ransacked aisle three. Stuffed animals, chew toys, and balls were scattered from one end to the other. The furry miscreant had even managed to stack four boxes of cat treats into a pile that looked like a set of stairs leading to the second shelf, where more items were in disarray. "Really, Rob. You couldn't have cleaned this up before you left?" she complained to herself. The parakeets, in their cages along the wall, squawked in agreement.

A knock rattled the accordion door leading to the mall. The same brown-uniformed delivery man as the day before stood outside with yet another box on a trolley. Joy signed for the package, and carefully carried the beat-up carton to the cash desk.

She didn't remember ordering a second shipment from NPU. When she read the manifest, her confusion cleared. North Pole Unlimited had sent her a complimentary display pack from their upcoming Christmas product line. Then she was surprised again. For the first time ever, the company's shipment was incomplete. The invoice listed twelve toys. The badly damaged package contained ten. Between the huge, missing piece in the side of the box and the tear at the bottom, Joy was surprised only two had fallen out during the trip.

She arranged the contents behind the desk. She needed to make a "Coming Soon" sign for them. Joy refused to put out any Christmas decorations before Halloween; it was an offense to decency. That didn't mean she wouldn't have another sign ready for November first.

An idea hit her as she straightened the rope-octopus's legs on the glass shelf. An unexpected box from NPU? Missing items? It was an excuse to call Decker Harkness. She could tell him about the shipment and the invoice over a coffee. She pulled his card out of her wallet, picked up her phone, and dialed before she had a chance to chicken out.

5. DECKER

DECKER HAD BARELY SETTLED behind his desk when his day took a turn for the better. Joy called. He agreed to meet her and was out the door before they finished their conversation.

The food court coffee was black, hot, and mellow. In other words, it was perfect. Joy's whipped-cream-topped, chocolate-drizzled cocoa made his teeth ache just looking at it. Decker was disappointed when she pulled a slip of paper from her purse. Apparently, she had a real reason to call him.

"North Pole Unlimited sent us a box of samples, but the shipment was incomplete. I thought your doll might be one of the missing ones. Do any of these product numbers match?" she asked.

He quickly scanned the list. The E.L.V.I.S. code Nick gave him didn't pop. Decker set the paper down to peruse again later. He might have missed it the first time. His eyes needed a chance to rest before he looked at the small type again, so he concentrated on the vision in front of him instead.

Decker had researched Joy's online history the night before, purely for professional reasons. No criminal history, upbeat, non-political public social media posts, and member in good standing of the Ottawa Humane Society. She might be one of the few people who were as honest as she looked. He still had trouble believing it.

The very sight of her made him smile. She looked like she had stepped off the page of *Girl Next Door* magazine with a bright blue sweater over a yellow T-shirt and jeans. She had a couple creases at the corners of her eyes, pushing her past the thirty-year mark, which was a good thing. He was thirty-eight himself; he didn't want to date out of his decade. Even if their coffee meeting was a bust in every other way, he was going to try to get a real date out of it.

"I'll have to double-check against the file I have at the office. Thanks for calling me about it. I was hoping to see you again," he said.

Joy blushed. "Did you have any luck at the other places you went?"

"No. Fins and Things was a dud. I also checked out Pure Bred, but my investigation there was inconclusive. I have to go back again." Joy's nose went up at the name of the second store. "You aren't a fan?"

"I would never speak badly of the competition, but if I did, I'd tell you that flea-infested pit of animal traumas is a disgrace of a pet store and a blight on the mall and world in general. I cannot recommend it for anything at all. And what they try to pass off as coffee cake is terrible," Joy said in an explosion of disgust.

"Don't hold back on my account." He knew from the second he met her, criminal or not, that she had good taste.

"My Dutch cinnamon coffee cake can take down their sawdust pucks any day of the week. I swear the sole reason they're still in business is because some people think they have to pay more to show how important they are and feel better about themselves. Did you know Pure Bred sells Funsters at thirty percent more than we do? There's no reason for that kind of markup," she continued.

"Unless you have customers stupid enough to pay it," Decker added.

"Exactly! See, you get it. I'd never sell a pet to some-body who shopped there. They'd treat a shelter animal like a second-class pet. I'm not saying animals are people too, but they are living creatures, not purse accessories you should dress to match your outfit."

"You know what? I'm going to keep mum about my next visit so I don't set you off," Decker said with a laugh. Her passionate responses were making him smile, but she was giving off clear signs she'd be equally as passionate if he were the one to annoy her.

Joy blushed again. "It might be safer," she agreed.

"Can I ask you why you hate them on our next date?"

"Is this our first date?"

"I hope so."

"And we're having another one?" she asked.

"Absolutely. Tonight?"

"I'm free tonight."

She hadn't made him work for it at all. That was a good sign.

She checked her watch, and Decker reluctantly let her get back to the store. He took a picture of the invoice first, planning to verify the model numbers with Nick.

But he spent most of the drive back to his office figuring out where to take Joy for dinner.

6. JOY

JOY DIDN'T MEAN to act scatterbrained for the rest of her shift, but the prospect of dinner with Decker threw her into a tizzy. Joy hadn't thought she was out of practice when it came to dating, but when she counted back the weeks since she'd had one with a promising guy, she was surprised to realize snow had still been on the ground.

But that was no reason for Spooky to nip at her after she gave the trio a scoop of doggy kibble in their food dish by mistake. Joy switched it to the proper food and was rewarded with a head-butt before she was completely ignored.

"Joy, did you place the order for more lint roller tape?" Rob called from the cash desk.

"You bet," she shouted back. She hadn't. They didn't carry lint rollers, let alone the tape. It was a code they'd developed for shoplifters. The young man with the potential sticky fingers wasn't hard to spot. Jeans so stiff they could stand up by themselves, a dark fleece hoodie with creases in the arms and across the chest, and a ball cap pulled low over his glasses. He looked like he was out to rob the place and had bought new clothes to do it.

He wasn't there for anything of value. Kitten Caboodle had pricy items, but those were the twenty- or fifty-pound bags of food, not anything he could slip under his sweater. The smaller stuff wasn't worth the effort, although that didn't mean she and Rob let it slide.

Joy approached him from behind as he moved into the aisle with the various pet cages. Spooky, Midnight, Stinky, and Pumpkin were in their glass playpen. Half a dozen guinea pigs were scattered through three of the terrariums along the wall, and four parakeet cages hung from the ceiling, letting the birds keep watch over the entire store.

The guy darted furtively from side to side as he approached the cats' box. Joy pounced while his hand was moving toward the latch. "Can I help you?"

He jumped. "I was just looking!"

Maybe it was a prank; he was too inept to be shoplifting for profit. "I can see that. Can I help you find anything?"

"I want to adopt a cat. These black ones are cute. Are they Bombays?"

"If they are, we'd never be able to prove it. Their mother may have been but we don't have any papers for her. She was all black with golden eyes, but she didn't have a chip and was dropped off anonymously. The father was unknown."

"I want one," he said.

"Unfortunately, these kittens aren't fully weaned, so they aren't on our adoption register yet. They should be available in early November." She hated to tell him even that much. Giving away the Spice Boys was going to break her heart. Joy wanted to hold on to them until the very last possible second. Technically, the kittens would be old enough for new homes the next week, but the shelter had a policy: no black cat adoptions in October. Neither she nor Rob had ever had a problem with people doing anything to black cats for Halloween, but they set the rule to ensure their streak continued.

"But I really want one now. Today," the college-aged customer insisted.

Joy studied the shoplifter-slash-wannabe-cat-adopter, looking further than his clothing. "Do I know you?" she asked. She was certain she did, although she couldn't put her finger on it. He was barely twenty, past the acne stage but not yet able to fill a full beard, so he'd settled for a wispy goatee. His entire presence gave her a biting-on-tinfoil feeling.

"No. But you could if you sold me a cat."

Was he flirting with her? The toothy smile he shot her confirmed her first impression. Yes, he was. He didn't stand a chance. Especially after she'd spent half an hour with a man who could express his interest without playing games.

"They aren't available until November. If you'd like to leave your name at the desk, we can start your paper-work, and you'll be able to pick up your new kitten early next month." Joy kept talking even though he was halfway down the aisle by the time she finished her first sentence.

"I'll come back," he said.

"Don't bother," Joy retorted, but he was gone.

7. DECKER

NICK KLASSEN WAS VERY interested in his briefing. Decker had never seen anybody perform a line-by-line analysis or be so insightful about an interim report. He was glad he'd made dinner reservations first, because at this rate, their video call was going to take the entire afternoon.

"In summary, you like Kitten Caboodle as a store, but you think Pure Bred is more likely to have received it?" Nick asked.

"Yes. Joy, the Kitten Caboodle manager, has been very up-front with me about shipments. She even called me to do a follow-up. I get a good vibe from her. I've removed them from my list of potential locations. If she knew about the doll, she'd have told me," Decker said.

"What about Pure Bred?"

Hinky was not a professional term. But that's what it was. The whole store was one big question mark. "I'm still looking into them. I have a second visit scheduled for tomorrow." Decker wanted to know more about the secret cats he'd been offered. He also wanted a chance to search the premises himself. He didn't trust Liam or Lorraine to let him know if E.L.V.I.S. came in.

Klassen conferred with somebody off-screen. "Okay. Keep me informed. It seems like Pure Bred was already on our radar for shipment problems. If we get any information on this end, we'll forward it immediately. Good luck."

Decker headed home for a shower before returning to the mall to pick Joy up from work. He'd made reservations at Casa Roma.

Despite her text saying she'd be ready and waiting, she was neither. He found her petting the crying orange kitten who'd attacked him the day before. The three others in the cage were crying as well. He could swear he saw tears in their eyes. "What happened?" The kittens were the most pathetic things he'd ever seen.

"Rob decided it was time for them to be chipped. Nobody is happy about it."

The orange one abandoned Joy and her gentle strokes and toddled over to Decker's hand, which was dangling at the ledge. "*Yeow!*"

"Is that cat for 'pet me'? Or is it a warning he's about to leap on me again?" Decker asked.

"Pumpkin wants cuddles. Just avoid between his shoulders. Patting him on the head should work. Did you want to stay here with these guys while I grab my purse?"

"No problem." They weren't dogs, but the kittens were affectionate. The littlest black one tried to push Pumpkin away to get his own head-scratches. Decker ended up with two handfuls of kittens.

"They're never going to let you leave now," Joy said upon her return.

He pulled his hands from the case and ignored the

mournful mews. He barely heard them at all over the ringing in his ears. Joy may not have had time to go home, but she'd definitely taken the time to freshen up. She'd swapped her practical, short-sleeved golf shirt for a clingy, dark-red sweater and a long chain with a bauble at the end.

"Is this okay? You never texted me where we were going."

He knew he'd forgotten something. "Casa Roma. I hope you like Italian."

"I love Italian."

"What about the cats?"

"I'll come back and pick them up when we're done," Joy said.

It was a short drive to the restaurant. The hostess showed them to a semi-circular booth in the back. Decker followed Joy onto the bench and scooted around with her, not letting her put an empty place setting between them. He gave her room when she started gesticulating with a breadstick while telling him about her first trip to the symphony, but after that he shifted close again. Whenever she pushed her hair back over her shoulder, Decker caught a hint of something sweet and floral. It was intoxicating. So much so, he realized he'd missed Joy's question.

"Sorry?" Decker asked.

"I was wondering how you got into the private-eye business. It seems like a big jump from police officer to self-employed detective."

"There were parts of being a cop I really liked. And parts I didn't. Working for myself, I get to concentrate on the parts I like."

"Like hunting down missing dolls?"

"Admittedly, some of my jobs aren't very exciting. On

others, I get to meet some amazing people." Beautiful, intelligent, funny people. He was seriously considering asking Joy on a third date when they were halfway through their second, but he didn't want to scare her off. "Can I ask you a question?"

Joy made a "go ahead" motion as she took a sip of her diet cola.

"If you're worried about Pumpkin, Spooky, Stinky, and... and..."

"Midnight," she supplied.

"Midnight being adopted by a stranger, why don't you adopt them yourself? Unless you already have enough animals," he added. He could easily see her as a crazy cat lady—the sexy kind, not the grandmotherly, doily-and-slip-covered-sofa kind.

"Believe me, I want to. Unfortunately, my life is too transitory right now. When I took the managerial job at Kitten Caboodle, I told Rob it was going to be for six months, until I finished my veterinary assistant diploma. But then I couldn't get hired on anywhere else with it. That was two years ago."

"You didn't want to get a pet in case you couldn't afford to keep it? That's responsible."

"That's part of it. I've been leasing my apartment month to month as well, in anticipation of moving to my new job. I got my landlord to agree to let me bring the kittens into the building to be fostered until they were weaned, but the deal was for eight weeks and not a day longer. The kittens are permanent shelter residents after this weekend until we can find them homes."

"That's pretty impressive. You've worked at Kitten Caboodle for two years and haven't adopted anything yet. I figured you were a soft touch," Decker teased.

"I stayed strong until Pumpkin and the other Spice Boys arrived. I don't know what I'm going to do now. They need a good home."

Decker didn't understand the look that flashed across her face, but he smiled when she leaned into him with fake puppy-dog eyes. He outright laughed when she grabbed her bottom lip and jiggled it to make it look like it was trembling.

"Stop it. No! I'm not taking a kitten home with me. I'm not a cat guy." A kitten would totally ruin his street credit. Especially an orange crybaby. Maybe one of the black ones, if it promised to act aloof and mysterious when clients were in the office. Giving people head-butts for scratches was not the act of a P.I.'s cat. "I'm certain you'll make sure they all go to good homes. In fact, I'd bet on it."

She smiled. "You'd bet right."

Joy tried to decline dessert, but Decker caught the sparkle in her eye when the waitress mentioned the tiramisu. He ordered it for her. He wasn't a fan but it was worth it to watch Joy enjoy it.

He drove her back to the mall, taking an obviously out-of-the-way route to stretch out the ride. She directed him to the back of the building, and he pulled to a stop beside a battered pickup which was parked in front of a steel security door.

"Thank you for a lovely dinner," Joy said. She didn't make a move toward the door handle.

"I had a great time," Decker responded. That was an understatement. He hadn't laughed so hard in months.

She turned to face him full on. "Me, too." She shifted her hand to the center console.

He wasn't going to get a clearer signal than that.

Decker licked his lip as he leaned closer. Joy tilted her head and did the same. Then she pulled away, staring at the back of the building. "That's not right."

"What's not?"

"The door."

He walked her to the building. Under normal circumstances, most of his motivation would be chivalry; it was late, and the area was poorly lit. The fact he got to hold her hand was strictly secondary. This time, he went with her for protection. "Look," she said.

No wonder she'd noticed it. Something, or someone, had scratched all the paint away from the handle.

"Something's wrong."

8. JOY

THE REAR DOOR led into the shelter half of Kitten
Caboodle. The back room, where the animals were
kenneled, opened into the play room at the front where
they wandered at will. A wall of windows with a gate in
the doorway looked from the playroom into the store,
allowing people to check out the pets available for adoption. The mall entry was on the store half. As soon as mall
hours ended, a set of accordion doors closed, locking the
place down tight.

Not that she had a chance to show him any of that.
She thought Decker would come inside with her to check
things out. Instead, he backed her away from the door and
locked her in his car while he called the police.

It was ridiculous. If there had been an intruder, the
animals would have been going nuts. They would have
heard them, even through the door. But, no, Decker
wouldn't let her collect her poor kitties.

He reached over and picked her hand out of her lap.
"The cats are probably sleeping. You said so yourself. A

few more minutes isn't going to make any difference." He gave her fingers a squeeze. "They'll be fine," he repeated.

The Ottawa Police Service arrived quickly, and the responding officers did a walk-through. As soon as they gave the go-ahead, she yanked her hand from Decker's and fumbled with the car door. Decker grabbed her again as she hurried to the shelter. "Take it easy or you'll freak out the cats."

What really annoyed her was that he was right. Getting them upset wouldn't help anybody. Decker's being right didn't make her like him any better. Somebody had broken into her store while her babies were there. That required a certain level of freaking out.

"Breathe." His order was gentle, but unmistakable. "The kittens are okay. You're okay. We'll load them up and I'll move them to your truck while you deal with the police." He rubbed his thumb over the back of her hand as he escorted her to the pair of uniformed officers waiting inside.

He introduced her to the two men, and then a burly black man appeared on the scene.

"Charlie? What are you doing here? You don't do break-ins," Decker said.

"I heard your name on the radio and figured things were going to be interesting. And they are. Introduce me to your friend."

"Joy, this is my former partner, Inspector Charlie Barr. Charlie, this is Joy McCall. She's the assistant manager here and was coming back to pick up some things before heading home for the night when we noticed someone had tried to jimmy the door."

"Miss McCall, we've cleared the store, if you want to go in," Charlie said. "Decker, I need a minute."

Spooky and Midnight raised their wee heads when they heard her voice, but immediately burrowed back under their blanket. Stinky *meeped* at her until she picked him up for a cuddle. Pumpkin launched himself at Decker when he joined them. If the man didn't clue in to the fact he'd been adopted, Joy was going to have to explain it to him. His subconscious seemed to know. Decker settled the kitten in the crook of his arm while he gave his statement.

The would-be robbers never made it inside. Nothing was missing. The worst of it was the birds were squawking non-stop at being awoken late in the evening. People might call them songbirds, but there was little more grating than a chorus of shrieking parakeets and cockatiels.

Joy stopped at the end of the toy aisle and stared. Someone had made a mess of the stuffed animals again. It was like an arm had swept them off the shelves into the middle of the floor. Rob would never have left them there, even if he'd been cleaning and the mop had gotten away from him. Especially after the strip she'd torn off him the last time.

She pointed them out to Decker's friend. "That's not right. I'm sure Rob will say he didn't put those there, and everything was shipshape when he left for the night. But..."

"But what, Joy?" Even when he was chatting with his cronies, Decker was never more than a couple steps away. He lifted Pumpkin from his arms and laid him over Joy's shoulder. The purr in her ear eased the tension in her neck.

"But if the robber didn't take anything tonight, and

this happened last night too, does that mean somebody is hiding in the shelter?" she asked.

Then she was outside, with two cats in her arms, and Decker was beside her with Spooky and Midnight in a kennel. Joy loaded all four kittens into the carrier and tucked it into her passenger seat. Then she waited for the police to search the store and shelter again. She wasn't surprised when they came up empty.

When they finally let her back in, Joy noticed one more thing. Light from the mall shone through wide cracks in the accordion security door. Cracks that hadn't been there when she'd opened the store that morning.

"I can't explain that," Decker said. "Maybe they tried to gain access through the mall first."

Eventually the police let her go home, but only after she agreed to show up at the station to give a full statement the next day—later that morning, she corrected in her head.

"I'm following you home," Decker said.

"You don't have to. I've kept you up too late as it is." The mall closed at eight. Rob left at nine. Decker had driven her back to her car at eleven. That felt like days ago.

"Joy, I'm following you to your place. A break-in, or even an attempted break-in, is traumatic. You're going to crash when the adrenaline wears off. Let me make sure you get home safely." He was holding her hand again. A cold gust of wind blasted through the narrow parking lot, sending dead leaves skittering along the curb. The chilly air hit her sweat-damp sweater and a shiver escaped. Another followed, and suddenly Joy was vibrating with cold and emotion.

Maybe he had a point. "My apartment is in Stittsville." Over thirty minutes away.

"I won't lose you. Buckle up."

The streets were deserted. She pointed to the visitor stalls at the other end of her building. Decker still managed to meet her halfway up the sidewalk.

"I wasn't expecting company," Joy apologized in advance. She tried to picture what she'd find when she opened the door. She remembered the teacup and cereal bowl on her coffee table. She'd forgotten about the plate covered in coffee cake crumbs from her Netflix binge-watch the night before. A pair of gym socks hung over the arm of her recliner, and two entwined throw blankets were pooled on the ottoman. Overall, it wasn't bad.

The kittens were used to having free run of Joy's kitchen, so she opened the carry-kennel's door in case they wanted to wander during the night, and locked the baby gate leading into the hall. All four kittens were out cold when she paused to check on them before she returned to the living room. At least somebody would sleep that night.

She felt Decker's chest brush against her back. He looked over her shoulder. "See, they're fine."

"I'm not crazy. Somebody was in the store with them."

"I know you're not crazy. That pile of toys was freaky. Harmless, but freaky. Do you want me to check your apartment?" he offered.

She was a big girl and a rational person. There had been no signs of a break-in at her home. She ought to say no. There was a security door to get into the building, and the deadbolt on her door had been engaged.

"Stay here. I'll take a peek." Decker returned two

minutes later. "All your windows are locked, and there was nothing under your bed except a whole bunch of balls with bells in them. I left them there," he reported.

She blinked and he was right in front of her. "How are you doing?" he asked.

"Fine."

"Joy. How are you doing?" He used his command voice again.

"I'm a little freaked, a lot tired, and angry our date was ruined." It should have been illegal for dates to go so well. Then some faceless burglar had stolen it from them.

Decker's blue eyes darkened at her words. Joy would have worried if not for the huge smile on his face. "I'm glad you had such a good time. I don't think the date was ruined."

"We spent two hours talking to the police. I realize they were friends of yours but how can you say this date ended successfully?"

"Because it hasn't ended yet."

"Would you like to go out with me again?" Joy asked breathlessly.

"That's my line," Decker protested.

"You were taking too long."

"Dinner again tomorrow? Or is that too soon?"

"Dinner tomorrow sounds great." Or lunch, but that sounded a little desperate.

He leaned in to kiss her, and the kittens went wild. It was a conspiracy. "What's wrong with them?" Decker asked.

She blushed. She was such a bad kitten momma. "It's time for their bedtime snack."

"Can't they wait till I kiss you?"

A kitten quartet of pathetic meowing rang from the kitchen.

"Apparently not. Do you want to stay and help?" He could feed Pumpkin. It would be good practice for when he took the kitten home.

"I should go," he said quietly. "You have to give a statement and go to work tomorrow morning. And I have an early conference call I can't miss. Stop tempting me."

She was glad he sounded as disappointed as she did that their date was ending.

"I'll call you later to let you know our dinner plans."

"Okay," she whispered.

"Plan on something fancy."

She didn't know where they were going but she already had a dress in mind.

INTERLUDE

Late October
 North Pole Unlimited Headquarters

Nick leaned back in the chair he'd inherited from George. He'd also received the desk, the office, and the stuffed trout on the wall. He'd get rid of the fish. He was keeping the rest. George had said, "You need the space more than I do these days", and had removed himself to a temporary office down the hall. Now the nameplate on the door read "Nick Klassen, Vice-President of Human Resources" and it was time to live up to the title.

Jilly Lewis knocked on the open door. She'd started with the company working for George. She was ten years older than Nick, and had a son twenty years younger. As an experienced executive assistant, she had also come with the position. Nick could have hired someone new, but only an idiot would give up all her experience. Jilly kept him on track, even when he didn't know what was going on. "I have a schedule update for you," she said.

"Hit me."

"Adelaide pushed your meeting to this afternoon. Instead, you have video interviews all morning for Andrea's top choices. Your first is in ten minutes if you want to fix your hair."

He raised his hand automatically. "What's wrong with my hair?"

Jilly smirked at him and walked out.

Ten minutes later he was looking at the smiling face of a thirty-year old woman. She was fully made-up and dressed-up, even though it was only a video call. He liked that she took it so seriously. There weren't many personal indicators in the file Jilly had provided; she said the employment agency wanted to make the process as blind as possible as not to influence decisions on either side.

"Hello, Miss McCall. I'm Nick Klassen. Thanks for agreeing to meet this way."

"It's not a problem at all." Her voice wavered for a second before she coughed to clear her throat. "I'm glad I have the chance to talk to you."

"Why don't you tell me a bit about your background?"

"I have a veterinary assistant diploma from—"

Two and a half hours later, Nick ended his fourth and final interview of the morning. He took a lap around his desk, stretching his arm over his head, before he strode to the president's office. He wasn't surprised to find Dr. Andrea Farnsworth with his grandmother.

"How did it go?" Dr. Farnsworth asked.

"I think we've gone from four to two." He handed her the files of the two applicants he liked best. "Joy McCall has a lot of practical familiarity with animals, but not much experience on the lab side. Brent Farrin has the reverse problem. He's got a boatload of technical lab knowledge, but has done very little hands-on work. I think you'd be happy with either of them. You just need to know what you'll want them working on. Then we'll find out where they are and if they're willing to relocate. Do you have a preference?"

"I do." But that was all she told him.

His grandmother wasn't any help either. "Andrea and I will discuss things and get back to you. How is your hunt for our next security chief coming?"

He forced a smile. "Decker is hot on E.L.V.I.S.'s trail."

"He's got nothing?"

He deflated. "He's got nothing," Nick admitted. The detective was working hard; the sheer number of negative results from leads he'd followed was staggering, but what they needed was a positive one. It didn't help that Decker didn't have the complete story. Nobody wanted the full details of E.L.V.I.S.'s proprietary technology to leave the company, even if it left the detective stumbling around in the dark. "Decker is supposed to call with an update today, but I don't have high hopes for a recovery at the moment."

His grandmother winced. "That is unfortunate. Not about your candidate, about the prototype." She brightened slightly and added, "At least we know the "evade" feature works."

"Gram!"

9. DECKER

SOMETHING NIGGLED in the back of his brain about the attempted break-in at Kitten Caboodle, but until his subconscious decided to share, Decker couldn't do anything about it. What he could do was complete his investigation into Pure Bred.

But first.

"Good morning, Nick." Decker was back in his suit and tie. He wasn't dressed to impress his client, although it never hurt. He needed to make himself even more memorable at Pure Bred to get more information on their Funster shipments and their mysterious cat sales.

"Any news?" the vice-president asked.

"More questions than anything else. I'm going to lean on Pure Bred hard today. Until I know what they're hiding, I have to assume it's E.L.V.I.S. The prototype's GPS says it was somewhere in the mall. Someone must have it. I'll do another search today in the store and café in case I missed it or somebody moved it," Decker said.

He was reaching for his coffee cup when he caught a glimpse of Nick Klassen's face. The man winced and was trying to hide it, badly. Nick tried to get his usual grin back in place but his mouth kept twitching.

"What?" Decker demanded. The smallest additional detail could help him bust the case wide open. He didn't need clients who withheld information.

"It might have moved, but not because somebody moved it," Nick said.

"Explain."

"We did tell you the doll moved. That it had an animatronics component," Nick hedged.

"According to the specifications you sent, that meant it had articulating joints and the capability to wave its arms and turn its head."

Nick flinched on the screen. "Those specs might not have been entirely accurate. When we said it moves, we meant it can move itself. Walk. Climb. Curl up in a ball and hide."

"Why would you develop a doll that could do that?" Decker asked. "Nick, Mr. Klassen, what—specifically— did you hire me to find?"

The explanation did not improve Decker's temper. By the time their conversation ended, Nick's assistant Jilly had sent him the updated specification of what he was truly looking for.

Calling E.L.V.I.S. a doll was like calling a shotgun a pellet delivery system. The description was technically accurate but entirely and dangerously understated. How had they expected him to find their missing, highly advanced Electronic Long-range Video/audio Interactive Surveillance unit when he thought he was looking for an action figure?

Decker spent the rest of the morning familiarizing himself with E.L.V.I.S.'s true capabilities. The surveillance unit was supposed to replace North Pole Unlimited's current E.O.S. model, whatever that was. E.L.V.I.S.'s purpose was to observe its designated target, record where the subject was, what it was doing and who it was doing it with, and send the data back to NPU's security room via a satellite link. From there, the footage was redirected to whoever was owned the unit. Unfortunately for NPU, the satellite link and the geo-positioning system were on the same circuit, and both were malfunctioning. That meant while E.L.V.I.S. was in Archer Plaza, recording whatever it decided needed to be recorded, it also had the capability of following its subject from place to place. Decker was looking for a moving needle in a retail haystack.

He'd wasted enough time being covert. Something this sensitive needed more direct action.

His first move was to stop at the mall's customer service booth where he dropped off a flyer offering a reward for locating his "sick niece's missing dolly." If a mall employee didn't contact him directly for the obscene amount of money he was offering, the booth attendant would make sure he found out if and when E.L.V.I.S. was turned in.

He checked his watch. It was still too early to stop by Kitten Caboodle. Decker had texted Joy when he got up, to see if she'd slept well or if she'd had nightmares about the break-in. PTSD could happen even if she hadn't been in the shelter at the time. She texted back a "Fine. Thanks for asking. Looking forward to tonight!" and a bunch of smiley faces and emojis.

He read the text again while he fought against his instincts to go verify Joy's state of mind. "You can go after you finish at Pure Bred," he bargained with himself.

His shirt was spotless and his tie straight when he strode into Pure Brewed for the second time. "Black, drip, the largest you've got." He wasn't out to impress anybody this time. The barista didn't question him.

The café, he noted again, was sparsely decorated to just this side of "no personality whatsoever." A handful of generic prints of European street scenes littered the walls and some fake bamboo plants in plastic containers sat in the corners. Behind the cash register, two photographs of a Caribbean coffee estate were on display: an old one in sepia tones, and the other a more recent shot of the same view, showing the upgraded plant facilities while the same plantation house stood in the background. Everything else was café and store merchandise advertised on chrome and glass shelves. Not only was there no place to display a doll, there wasn't anywhere to hide one. Unless E.L.V.I.S. was behind the counter or in a storeroom—an unlikely option since a surveillance unit wouldn't monitor a mostly empty room—Decker had no choice but to move on.

Liam was working again. Good for Decker, bad for him. The twenty-something tried to duck into whichever row Decker wasn't searching. Not in the mood for games, Decker strode down an aisle at the other end of the store, then came up behind Liam when he was looking the other way. "Where's my cat?"

"Ummm."

"Where's your boss?"

"In the office. I'll take you," Liam said eagerly.

The kid knocked on the door, and Decker heard Lorraine before he saw her. "Liam, what are you doing back here? You should be on the floor."

"He's back. I'm gone."

The shelf stocker had no problem throwing his supervisor under the bus. It wasn't a great move when it came to future employment, but Liam would do well in a survival situation.

"Mr..." Lorraine let her voice trail off. Decker stared at her, and waited for her to admit she knew who he was. "Mr. Harkness, what can I do for you?" she asked.

"You could give me an update on the cat you promised me." Decker knew he was pushing hard, but he recognized her type. Lorraine wouldn't respond to anything other than direct confrontation. He proved himself right when she nodded.

"We haven't received them yet, but I did receive some pictures from our breeder." She pulled her phone out of her blazer pocket and called up a photo. She turned the screen to show him. "We'll have three males. You'll have first pick when they come in," she promised.

They looked a little like Joy's kittens, only bigger. Of course, since those were the only kittens he'd ever actually seen in person, he didn't have a lot to compare them to. Black was black. "They look big enough to be weaned," he said, repeating something Joy had said about her trio. He hoped it was a suitable observation for these cats.

"They have been. It's a transportation issue at this point," Lorraine explained.

It sounded like a weak excuse. "What about the Funster doll I'm looking for," Decker pressed.

"I told you. We don't carry anything like that."

"You also told me you didn't have any Bombay cats for sale the first time I spoke to you. I know the doll was sent to either Pure Bred or Kitten Caboodle," he lied. "I'm willing to pay a premium but I need to finalize the purchase within the week." It had hit him earlier he could kill two birds with one stone by having Lorraine turn her own store upside down looking for E.L.V.I.S., rather than spend his own time searching for the doll.

Lorraine's pupils dilated at the word "premium" but aside from that she did nothing to give away her interest. "If it was shipped to us in error, I'll give you a call if we locate it. If there's nothing else?"

Decker didn't waste time with goodbyes. He'd done what he wanted. He checked his watch on the way out. If he timed it right, he might be able to take Joy to lunch.

It was ridiculous he didn't like going twelve hours without seeing her. He had no idea who she was a week ago. It was too much. He was moving too fast. He didn't care. He had an interesting case and the prospect of lunch with a beautiful, intelligent woman. E.L.V.I.S. and Joy had come into his life at the time he'd needed them both. He'd give back the doll. He was keeping the girl.

10. JOY

JOY HAD KNOWN she was making a mistake when she did it, but it didn't stop her. She grabbed a handful of her silky knit sweater-dress and tugged it over her hips. The royal blue fabric was fine when she stood behind the till or lifted items on the upper racks, but whenever she squatted to reach something on the lower shelves, her dress rode up and became a mini. She only needed to tolerate it for four more hours until she was done for the day.

She shouldn't have worn it. It was a summer outfit, too thin for the autumn temperatures. But since she was in a climate-controlled building, she thought she could get away with it. Decker hadn't said he'd stop by during the day. In fact, he probably wouldn't since he had a job too, but if he did appear, she wanted him to see her favorite dress before she put it away for the season.

After she'd pulled the dress out of her closet, she'd lost half an hour trying to choose what she'd wear for her date that night. She'd have to make a decision when she got home. At the moment, she was pleased her matching heels were comfortable because she was being run off her feet.

After the grandma who wanted eight packets of cat treats for her darling Siamese's birthday party, the woman who couldn't decide which collar looked better on her poodle, and the three-year-old demon princess in the stroller who pulled six bags of birdseed off the shelf, Joy happily took a minute to ignore customers while she crouched to sweep the scattered seeds into a dustpan.

It was probably why the person in the next row didn't see her.

"How can I get you out of the store with me?" A man's voice floated over from the next aisle.

Joy wanted to cheer. He sounded like he was standing in front of Myrtle and Baron's cage. The birds had been surrendered when their owner was admitted to a long-term care facility. The parakeets were cheerful birds. She'd love it if they went to the same home.

"Good morning. Can I help you with…" Her question trailed into nothingness when she saw the guy from yesterday loitering next to the kittens' playpen. She felt her nose turn up as well, but that was a reaction to the cloud of body spray wafting her way. His hand darted away from the screen she'd placed on top of the glass box to keep strangers from touching the cats without permission. Exactly like he was trying to do. She'd even taped a sign to the glass: *If you want to pet the kittens, please ask an employee to help you. Kittens love supervised snuggles!* "Excuse me!" she said loudly. "Can I help you?"

The correct answer was no. Handsy guy didn't seem to understand that.

"I changed my mind. I want to put my name in to get

these three black Bombays. What do I need to do to get started?" he asked.

"As I told you yesterday, we offer no pedigree for these cats. If you'd like them anyway, we need your name and contact information, including a copy of your driver's license to put on the paperwork," Joy said. The shelter's adoption contract also gave them permission to run credit and criminal background checks. This potential cat-daddy might be legitimate but Joy would bet her next paycheck the fine print would scare him off.

He pulled a wad of cash out of his pocket and waved it in her face. "I'd rather give you a deposit and leave my number. I'll need them by the end of the week."

This special snowflake had no clue who he was dealing with.

"*Again*, as I told you *yesterday*, these kittens will not be available for adoption until *November*."

He started peeling off bills. "What's this really going to cost me?"

"Get. Out!"

Joy hadn't meant to be quite so loud. His eyes were already wide, and the magnifying lenses in his glasses gave him a comical air. She didn't let herself smile until he was out of the store.

Spooky and Midnight butted their heads against the glass until she caved and picked them up. Pumpkin covered his nose with his paws and sneezed. "Yes, Pumpkin, that rude man was wearing too much cologne."

She put the kittens down to let them scamper on the floor for a few minutes to stretch their little legs. Both of them darted halfway down the row and paused in front of a stack of fifty-pound dog food bags. They sat side by side and looked at the pile.

"That's not kitty food, you two." She took a box of cat treats from the cubby under their play box and shook it. "Want a snack?"

They didn't move. Their eyes were riveted to the shelf.

"Fine." Joy scooped them up and returned them to the display case. "Don't start whining," she told them when they peeped at her. "I gave you a chance to run around. You didn't want to. Now you can stay there while I go for lunch unless Rob wants to let you out."

Midnight peeped again and batted at her hand.

"Bad kitty."

"He's a baby. What did you expect?" Decker's warm voice filled her ears and made her head spin.

"Hey," was all she managed.

He leaned in and shook his finger at the kittens. "Are you monsters giving Joy a hard time?"

Pumpkin leapt at his hand, missed, and fell awkwardly on his side. Decker poked him gently in the belly and Pumpkin's legs flailed for a moment. He stopped and gave Decker a plaintive look. Decker poked the kitten once more, and the cat's legs started going again.

After the fifth time, Joy felt obligated to step in. "He's not going to stop doing that any time soon," she told Decker.

His mouth made an O and his hand froze in mid-tickle. It was like he didn't realize how long he'd been doing it. Joy already had a litter box and set of food and water dishes picked out for Decker and Pumpkin as an adoption gift for when Decker figured it out.

"I didn't expect to see you today. It's a pleasant surprise," she added before he got the wrong idea.

"I had some business in the mall. It's done. I thought I'd take you to lunch," Decker said.

"Instead of supper?" It made wearing the dress a good choice, but she wanted a long, romantic dinner, not a processed, food-court hamburger. The change of plans didn't necessarily mean anything bad. He might have to work unexpectedly or—

"No. And supper. Can you go now?"

"Rob, I'm on lunch!" Decker wrapped his fingers around hers and she was halfway out the door when she heard the responding "Okay."

Decker frowned at the spinach side salad and roll she got from Fresh-To-Go. "Is that all you're having?"

"It is if you're still taking me to a nice place tonight."

Decker pressed his lips together, but Joy saw the hint of a smile. She speared a forkful of greens. "Did you get what you needed at your meeting?"

"Not yet, but I will. How was your morning?" he asked before starting on his first cheeseburger.

"Busy, with a little weird thrown in for good measure."

He set down his burger. "Tell me."

"The kittens are being odd, even for cats. They're constantly freezing and staring at the bags of kibble across the aisle," she said.

"Maybe they're hungry."

"Oh, they're always hungry. But you know what? Now that I think about it, those shelves are directly behind the aisle where somebody keeps knocking all the toys to the floor. Maybe something's there." Joy spoke slowly, forming each word as the idea crystalized in her head. The shelf was too small for a person, but something else using it as a hiding place was entirely possible.

"Eat," Decker ordered.

Joy picked up her fork. "Not a mouse. That's too small. You don't think it's a rat, do you? The back door to the shelter is always being opened and closed, and the garbage bins are stored at the corner of the parking lot a few stalls down from us. A raccoon, maybe?"

"Eat. We'll take a look when I walk you back to the store."

"You don't have to—" His look shut her up. "We'll look after lunch," she agreed.

11. DECKER

HE FOUND A SHOE. A shoe roughly an inch and a half long, made of a soft, fuzzy, navy rubber Decker could bend in half between the tips of his thumb and forefinger. He examined it closely, then put it back where he found it.

That was one question answered. E.L.V.I.S. had been shipped to Kitten Caboodle, although there was no sign of it at the moment. Decker didn't know if it was good or bad news. He had proof E.L.V.I.S. had chosen Joy's store, and one aisle in particular, as its home base. It didn't answer his second question about whether or not the doll had moved on after causing back-to-back nightly mischief which had put its hidey-hole into jeopardy. Or his third, where he wondered if it was what had damaged the store's mall doors.

At least he had something to report to Nick Klassen. After days of no leads, any progress was an improvement. Finding E.L.V.I.S.'s old lair was a solid mark in the good-investigative-techniques column. Finding his new one would be even better.

Now Decker had to figure out what the doll was doing. E.L.V.I.S. was a surveillance unit, designed to spy on whatever subject its programmers designated. Who or what was E.L.V.I.S.'s target?

"Did you find anything?" Joy asked.

Decker heaved the dog food bags back into place. "No trace of any animals," he prevaricated. He didn't want Joy to worry that rats or other vermin infested her store, but he couldn't tell her the truth. "Will you let me know if it happens again?"

He read the independent streak on her face. She was going to say no. She wouldn't want to bother him about some stupid mess at her job. He frowned, knowing that solving this mystery was one more problem she added to her list of responsibilities when it was his, and he already had the solution. "Okay," she said, but there was a slight hint of resentment to it.

"I know you can handle yourself but I worry," Decker said.

"Don't."

"But I like worrying about you." Evidently, that was the right argument to make.

"Fine," she said with a huff.

"Great. I'll see you tonight."

Right after he made his report.

Nick Klassen looked surprisingly serious considering the positive nature of Decker's news. "What do you mean, it wasn't there?"

"E.L.V.I.S. wasn't there. The shoe I found matched the one the doll was wearing in the photos you sent, but the unit itself was missing. You told me it was designed to do surveillance. Was it programmed when it left your facility?"

Decker hadn't realized cameras embedded in laptops were sensitive enough to catch pupil dilation and skin tone changes until he saw Nick turn a ghostly shade of white, then green. "Why do you ask?"

Evasion wasn't a good sign. "Mr. Klassen. Nick," he said, trying to sound friendlier. "I get the feeling you aren't being completely honest with me. I can't help you if you hold things back. Was E.L.V.I.S. programmed when it arrived in Ottawa?"

Nick gulped. "Yes."

Now they were getting somewhere. "To track a particular person?"

"No. It has standard programming to respond to a list of illegal behaviors. Violence and theft primarily. If E.L.V.I.S. recorded something that fell within its parameters, its default settings would have kicked in."

"I'm going to need to know the doll's responses if I have a hope of catching it now that we know it's on the move," Decker said.

"I'll have to check with the I.T. department. In the meantime, keep looking. I think you're right. E.L.V.I.S. will likely return to that spot. It's too bad you didn't slip a little tracker into his shoe. He's programmed not to leave any trace of himself behind. Report back tomorrow with any progress you've made. I'll have an answer for you about the rest."

Decker happened to have a miniature GPS tracker. However, in this case, miniature was a relative term. It was still larger than the doll's shoe. He'd have to think about his options.

Tomorrow.

Tonight was for dining and romancing. And dancing if Joy absolutely insisted.

When he picked her up, Decker hoped she would insist. The blue dress she'd worn to work was heart-stopping, but this one was even better. It was an iridescent rusty red with long sleeves and a neckline scooping low under her collarbone. He helped Joy into her coat, said good-bye to the cats—Pumpkin twice—and walked her to his truck.

Joy didn't waste time ordering a salad. She went for the steak—rare, twice-baked potato with cheese, and the steamed broccoli, which she pushed out of the way with her fork. She also helped him split a bottle of red wine.

Decker was a big enough guy that two glasses of wine over three hours wouldn't affect him. Joy was slighter. She laughed a little louder when she started her second glass, and her brown eyes shone a bit brighter. She told him about Pumpkin's adventures since he'd arrived at the shelter. He told her about how his knee was too bad to pass the department's physical for returning to work. Then they got into music and movies. The conversation never died.

"Dessert? Coffee?" the waiter interrupted.

Joy's eyes went wide at the offer, but she pinched her lips together and shook her head.

"Give us a minute," Decker ordered.

Once they were alone again, he nudged the dessert menu toward her. "They have some amazing desserts. The raspberry chocolate cheesecake is really good," he teased, wiggling the card to draw her attention to it.

"I'm too stuffed to enjoy it right now. If you'd like to come back to my place for coffee, by the time it's ready, I might have room. If you're interested." She looked at him over the top of her wine glass.

When the waiter returned to the table, their seats

were already cold. Decker left him a huge tip, though.

12. JOY

SHE SHOULD HAVE BAKED another cake. She and Decker each had a piece with coffee, and then another with their refills an hour later. She'd sent the last piece home with him to have for breakfast.

She stared into the mirror as she brushed her teeth. She'd given away cake. That was a serious declaration on her part. She must like Decker more than she'd been willing to admit to herself. She retreated a mental step and tried to look at Decker from the outside.

Handsome, funny, polite. Super interesting job. Protective, but still respecting the fact she could take care of herself.

She needed to take a bigger step back.

She shouldn't get too attached. They'd only had three dates; one was barely a coffee date, one had ended badly, and the other had been too perfect for words. She needed to slow down.

Joy wasn't even certain she was going to be around for much longer. The employment agency had contacted her again. They informed her that the employer had been impressed with her first interview and would be in touch if they wanted to move forward.

She was tempted to blow it off. Part of that was fear; new things were scary. She wasn't working in her dream job, but overall, her life was going pretty well at the moment. Joy wasn't sure she was willing to risk it all on an unknown, if they did eventually make her an offer.

On the other hand, she was already at ninety percent certainty about Decker. He was smart, handsome, funny, kind, and honest. The kittens also liked him; she trusted their judgment almost as much as her own. She had to figure out her priorities.

Sadly, he was giving her all the time she needed. When she'd asked him when they were going to see each other again, he'd frowned.

"I have to work. I'm pretty sure I'm going to be on a stakeout for the next few days, which flips me onto a night shift. It may take a while for me to find what I'm looking for," Decker told her, his voice gentle.

"Okay." She wanted a night to think things over, not a week-long break.

"No, it's not. My timing is terrible. If I can find another way to get this job done, I will, but until then I'm stuck. It does have one perk, though."

"What?" Joy couldn't think of a single good thing about not being able to see him at all for an indefinite period.

"Your breakfasts will be at the same time as my dinners. I can be your alarm clock and wake you up every morning. How would you feel about a personal coffee delivery service?"

She smiled. If there was only one benefit to Decker's new hours, it was a good one.

13. DECKER

THE CATS GAVE him the idea. Decker was stuck on how to track E.L.V.I.S. since a normal GPS chip wouldn't work. When he'd played with Pumpkin earlier, he'd felt the tiny microchip embedded in the cat's scruff. It was slightly larger than a grain of rice, which was the perfect size to be glued onto a doll shoe. Tracking it would be more difficult, but it was a start.

Decker spent his morning hunting down a suitable substitute, and finally located one thanks to a friendly vet who owed him a favor. A trip to the hardware store took care of the glue. Then he crashed on his office sofa for an afternoon nap until it was time to head to Archer Plaza.

He specifically timed his visit to the mall for after Joy left for the day to avoid any awkwardness. Now his plan rested on whether or not E.L.V.I.S. was fond of his blue fuzzy shoes.

Decker knew where to look. Luckily, the shoe was where he had left it. He quickly attached the microchip, then replaced the shoe on the corner of the shelf. He'd just finished shifting the bags of kibble back onto the shelf when Joy's boss came over.

"Can I help you find anything?"

Decker picked up a gold-tone pen from the floor, where he had placed it in case he got caught. "I came in to see if Joy was working, but apparently she's not. Then I dropped my pen and it rolled under the dog food. I got it, thanks."

Rob nodded. "You're Joy's friend," he said. It wasn't a friendly observation. "We—my wife and I—are Joy's friends too. She's a wonderful person and a great employee."

"I can't judge her work skills, but I think she's wonderful too. I've told her so," Decker said. He didn't appreciate being questioned about his intentions, but it spoke well for Joy that she had people who wanted to watch her back.

"Joy says you might be getting one of her cats. She wouldn't let them go to just anybody," Rob admitted.

"I'm getting a cat?" Decker repeated. What was going on this week with people thinking he wanted a feline sidekick? No self-respecting private detective had a cat—not in books, not in movies, and certainly not in real life. He hadn't given Joy the slightest clue he was interested in adopting a pet.

"She said Pumpkin had adopted you. But don't tell her I told you so."

The orange kitten was cute but that didn't mean Decker was going to take him home. "Don't worry. I don't intend to bring up any part of this conversation. I don't want to give Joy any ideas."

"I won't mention it either," Rob said with a laugh.

Decker slipped the pen into his jacket pocket and

patted the chip tracker that was already there. "Have a good night," he said before he exited into the mall.

Decker doubled back after a couple stores, until he was beside Kitten Caboodle's display window. He pulled the tracker from his pocket and turned it on, being careful not to jiggle the freshly soldered wires which were attached to a new motherboard. The upgraded technology was supposed to make the unit strong enough to read the microchip from a distance. He walked by the front door to make it work, proving his range was about sixty percent of what he'd hoped for. It was better than nothing.

He headed for the security office. One of Archer Plaza's night watchmen was a friend of a friend, who'd been told Decker was a former cop doing research for a novel. Decker was allowed to accompany the guards on their rounds. It wasn't the night he wanted to have. Not by a long shot.

"Getting settled in? Thermos of coffee? Binoculars? Box of donuts?" Joy texted him as the sound system announced shoppers had fifteen minutes before the mall closed. He laughed, if only because his hand had been in the box of donuts he'd brought for the guys when his phone went off.

"Check and check. Good day?" he sent back.

"Not bad. Crashing now. Late night last night "

Decker made the rounds three times without incident. The fourth gave him pause. He stopped outside the accordion doors leading into Kitten Caboodle. One of the sections was missing a six-inch piece of clear plastic along the bottom. It wasn't person-sized, but a doll could easily use it as a way into the store—or out of it. Decker pulled out his tracker. If the doll were inside, the unit would register the chip on the boot.

It didn't. E.L.V.I.S. was on the move.

Ten minutes further into his security sweep, he knew E.L.V.I.S. hadn't left the building. He didn't even need the tracker to confirm it. The doll was safely ensconced behind Pure Bred's glass security doors. Decker saw the surveillance unit marching up and down the rows inside, pausing every once in a while, then moving on.

If E.L.V.I.S. wasn't still in the shop or café when it opened the next day, Decker would have to start over again in Kitten Caboodle. There were worse places to be.

14. JOY

JOY GROWLED as she slipped her truck into reverse and made a second run at the narrow spot at the far end of the parking lot. She'd forgotten schools were closed for the day, which meant the mall would be the gathering place for every high school student in the capital area. In other words, it would be filled with annoying teenaged girls squealing *"Oh my Gooooood, they are soooo cuuuute! Can I pet them, pleeeeeeease?"* as soon as they saw the animals in the playroom.

She'd had a terrible morning. She'd set her alarm an hour earlier than normal, planning on a call from Decker for a breakfast date. It never came. She ended up wolfing down a pair of frozen waffles before she raced out the door.

"Come on, my preciouses. Into the store with you," she told the four yowling kittens in the carrier as she hefted it out of her passenger seat. The wind bit through her coat like it wasn't there, announcing fall was finally over. She'd be surprised if there wasn't snow on the ground by the end of the day. A particularly vicious gust caught her, and the carrier flew sideways. Four little thumps hit the plastic wall, and the feline howling increased. "Sorry, babies. It's a little rough out here."

She smiled for the first time that day when she got inside. "I'd swear it was you but I locked up last night," was Rob's greeting.

"Huh?" Joy winced at her inelegant response. She was too busy concentrating on removing the stubborn kittens and transferring them to their play space.

"The toys. In the aisle. It happened again. Now I know why you were annoyed. It took forever to get them cleaned up."

"Why are you here early?" she asked.

"It's a school holiday. We're going to have a crazy day."

The morning wasn't bad, but things picked up at lunch. It started with a trickle. A trio of teens politely inquired where the pet toy aisle was. Then a woman in a suit. Then a high school couple who walked in with their hands literally in each other's back pockets.

The businesswoman made it to the counter first. She set down a Funster sock monkey, a package of balls with bells in them, and a coupon authorizing her to one free Funster toy under twenty dollars. A coupon issued by Kitten Caboodle that Joy had never seen before. "I'm sorry but this voucher isn't valid," Joy told her customer.

"Of course, it is."

Joy scanned the barcode and showed the woman the resulting "unreadable" code.

"This is ridiculous. It's false advertising. I don't want the balls then, either."

Joy tossed both items on the shelf behind the register and turned around to find the teens already at the counter. "We want these," they chorused, putting down three identical mice in different-colored dresses.

She'd barely picked up the first when Joy was hit by a tsunami of noise. A mob of kids stretching as far as she could see tried to force its way into the store. "What on earth? Rob!"

"It's okay. You don't need to ring them up," the middle girl said. She handed over three coupons and the girls grabbed their toys and headed for the front door.

"Wait a minute. These coupons are fake. If you leave, that's theft!" Joy shouted at their backs.

They glanced over their shoulders, saw she was stuck behind the counter by the sudden influx of customers, and began pushing their way to the exit.

"Rob, stop those girls! They're stealing!" Joy yelled. Then she raised her voice even louder. "Attention everybody in Kitten Caboodle. The coupons for free Funsters are not real. They are fakes. Anybody trying to leave with a toy they did not pay for will be charged with shoplifting." Joy was never more grateful they'd programmed mall security into speed dial on the store's phone. She was calling for them while she made her announcement.

She heard Rob yelling from the door, but it still took several minutes to regain control of the store. Joy collected every coupon she spotted and ended up with over fifty. The first few handfuls were grudgingly given. After repeating herself so often she lost track, customers started coming up to the till and throwing them on the counter. Joy asked one young man the question she'd been dying to ask. "Where did you get this?"

He shrugged, his flannel shirt fluttering in the exaggerated movement. "Some guy was handing them out in the food court. Why'd he do that if they aren't real?"

"I have no idea," Joy replied. She hadn't done much more than glance at them, but with this latest revelation, she took another look. They appeared professional: they had the store logo, the deal in big print, a bunch of small, smudged type at the bottom, and a bar code in the corner. If it had been for any other store, she'd have assumed it was legitimate as well.

"Joy?"

She didn't look up. "What, Rob?" Couldn't he see she was still swamped?

"Not Rob."

Wait. She recognized the voice. Tension drained from her shoulders like somebody pulled the plug when she saw Decker stride down the aisle. The grumbling customers surrounding her till may not have recognized him, but they responded to his air of authority. Joy collected the last of the fake coupons easily as the free toy seekers filed out of the store.

"What's going on in here?" Decker asked.

She wordlessly handed him a coupon and began collecting the abandoned toys she'd tossed beside the cash register. "What is this?" he asked.

"Apparently, some guy was in the food court handing them out. We managed to shut down the first wave, but I don't know how many Funsters have already walked out the door. We'll have to put up a sign, I guess, warning people." Her interest in signage waned when her new situation finally hit her. "What are you doing here?" Joy told herself she wasn't as pleased as she sounded; he had stood her up for breakfast without a word.

"I missed you this morning."

That was sweet. But he could have called. "I was around," she said as she snagged the last Funster.

"I should have called."

Joy held out a plush goldfish. "Help me put these things away before I check on the kitties. It got pretty hectic in here," she told him.

Joy jammed toy after toy back on the ransacked shelf. She and Rob needed to do a full inventory later to see how many had walked out the door. Decker handed her the stuffed fish but held on to the tail when she tried to pull it away. "I'll call next time," he said.

"Thank you." But then she smiled at him because he admitted he had messed up.

"I suppose I should visit Pumpkin while I'm here," Decker continued. "Since you think I'm going to be adopting him and all."

"Who said that?" Not her. She wanted Decker to come to that realization on his own. Besides, if she were going to lose Spooky, Midnight, and Stinky, it would be nice to know she'd be able to check in on one of her babies.

"Why don't you go say hello and I'll be there soon to check on them?" Joy suggested.

She wasn't a minute behind him, but it was long enough to hear Decker say, "Since when did you start separating Pumpkin and the terrible trio? Where are they?"

"They're in the same case where they always are," Joy shouted back.

"No, they're not," he called from the other aisle.

Joy fought off a shiver. "Yes, they are." Stinky and Pumpkin had been fighting over a catnip mouse the last time she'd seen them; Pumpkin had been trying to shake Stinky off the tail.

"No, Joy. They aren't here."

15. DECKER

JOY HAD Pumpkin clutched to her chest in a grip she wouldn't be loosening any time soon. Decker knew this because he was holding Joy the same way. "Breathe," he ordered. Her shoulders trembled uncontrollably as she drew in another breath, making a pained noise that shook him to his core. He hated that sound. "I need you to pull it together so we can find the terrible trio. You can do this, Joy. I know you can."

She shouldn't have to. Decker had no doubt the fake coupons and resulting rush of customers were the setup. The kittens were the score, although he had no idea why. They were the feline equivalents of mutts; they had no value.

"I'm sure they're okay," he said.

"What if the kidnapper hurts them? Halloween is coming," she answered.

"What does that have to do with—really?" That was an actual thing? Decker had worked his fair share of Hell Nights and Halloweens but the most he'd ever dealt with was a few arson cases and some drunks being terrified of the decorations at a haunted house party. He assumed stories about black cats and Halloween were urban legends or Hollywood creations.

"We've never had any trouble, but we don't sell black cats in October, just in case. That's what I told the guy."

"What guy?" Now they were getting somewhere.

"The guy! The guy who wanted all three of them. I'm sure I told you about him. The one who came in three times this week and asked if Spooky, Midnight, and Stinky were up for adoption."

"No, Joy, you've never mentioned him," Decker said. He needed her to calm down.

She took a breath. "This guy wants my cats. When I told him they wouldn't be available until November, he got mad. He even offered me a bribe. I ordered him out of the store last time when he propositioned me," she said.

"Can you describe him?" It wouldn't be hard for Decker to get access to the mall's security camera system, especially when an actual crime had occurred. He needed Rob to make an official report, the faster the better.

"College student. Brown hair, over-styled. Brown eyes. Coke-bottle lenses in his glasses." Decker started to get a funny feeling in the pit of his stomach. "An embarrassment of a goatee. A couple inches taller than me. I think I know him. I recognized him the first time he came in but I couldn't place him."

It was enough. Her description painted an unmistakable picture in his head. Pure Bred. Liam. The kid had promised Decker a purebred Bombay by the end of the week. He must have been the one to supply Lorraine with the photo. No wonder the kittens looked so familiar; they were. Liam had motive and access.

"Joy!" Rob was not a big man; he was as tall as Joy and

about fifty pounds heavier, although according to Joy it was all heart. He also had the voice of a drill sergeant when he was mad. He appeared at the end of the aisle holding a sheet of paper. "Why do we have an invoice for eleven thousand dollars from North Pole Unlimited for a Funster doll?"

"It's obviously a mistake. How long have I worked for you? You know I'd never do anything like that. Can we find my missing kittens before you lay into me about someone else's clerical error?" Joy was getting over her shock and into fighting form by the sound of it. But if they didn't move quickly, her anger was going to swing back to despair and worry, and she'd lose the edge they needed to solve this case.

"You've called the police, right?" Decker asked.

Joy nodded. She wiped her eyes, smearing her makeup.

"Good," he continued. "Go to the bathroom. Splash some water on your face. Then give the description of that guy to the police officer who comes to take your report. Give whoever it is the case number you got after the break-in the other night. I have to go."

She shouldn't be allowed to look at him like that. Like he'd broken her heart. "I might have a line on Spooky, Stinky, and Midnight, but I have to go now. Alone. As soon as I know anything for sure, I'll call you. I promise." He was asking a lot, and he knew it. He'd been in Joy's life for days. The cats had been there for months.

But she nodded at him and stepped back. "If you don't get the answers you want, I'm going to try. I don't care if you are an ex-police-officer private detective. If somebody knows something and they aren't cooperating, I promise I can be scarier than you."

"How about we save that for Plan B?" He had to get moving. Had to before her eyes teared up again, or she asked him to stay, because he would. For as long as she wanted. He gave Pumpkin a rub behind the ears and strode out the door.

He wanted to storm Pure Bred and demand they hand over the kittens but that wouldn't work. He might be able to intimidate Liam, but Lorraine wouldn't fold so easily. If she suspected anything was off, he had no doubt she'd get rid of the evidence. If he wanted to do it right, he needed a few minutes to prepare.

For the first time ever, Decker was glad he was in a mall. A quick stop at a men's store netted him a fresh shirt. He ducked into a public restroom to change and comb his hair. He looked like a man on a mission who would not be put off for any reason. Perfect. Liam wouldn't put up a fight, and Lorraine would hesitate. One opportunity was all he needed. He couldn't rush it, so he didn't enter through the store. He walked into Pure Brewed and stood in the slow line. When he finally made it to the counter, he ordered a large decaf vanilla latte. He'd give it to Joy if he finished quickly. Then he squeezed past the woman sitting by the store entrance who had dragged over a chair for her poodle.

The usual number of customers meandering through the store gave Decker time to look around before getting down to business. Charlie didn't make him wait long; once he spotted his back-up enter the store, Decker tapped the cell phone in his pocket and made his move.

He came up behind Liam, trapping the shelf stocker between him and the plainclothes officer at the other end of the aisle. "Liam, how are you doing? Do you know how I'm doing? Not well." Decker continued without giving the young man a chance to speak. "Do you know why I'm not doing well? Because I ordered a purebred Bombay cat from you a week ago and *I still don't have it.* Why don't I have my cat, Liam?"

He was pushing hard, but he had to. He had a bad feeling about the kittens being away from Joy for a minute longer than necessary.

"Back," Liam choked out. "They're in the back."

"Show me," Decker ordered.

Lorraine was there waiting. She gave him a close-lipped smile and waved her hand over a wire cage that was a single square foot big. The terrible trio were in it, looking worse for wear. The color-coded collars Joy had given them were missing. Decker was surprised he recognized them anyway: Spooky with his floppy ear, Stinky with the kink in his tail, and Midnight with that permanent sleepy look on his fuzzy face. "Are these the Bombays?" Decker asked.

"Yes."

"How much do you want?"

"Two thousand. Cash. You get first pick because of your persistent inquiries," Lorraine said.

"Are they chipped?" Decker asked. He squatted beside the cage, undid the door and reached in to pet them. The kittens crowded around his hand, silent and shaking. The stillness was wrong. They were supposed to be raising a ruckus. Spooky should be trying to lead the escape, and Stinky should be farting, and then spinning around trying to see where the smell was coming from.

Lorraine hesitated. *She doesn't know the answer,* Decker thought. "They're awfully young. Can they be chipped this early?" he asked.

"No, they can't, and no, they aren't. The breeder was

leaving that up to the owners. I do have the paperwork guaranteeing their pedigrees, though, if you'd like to see it."

"Yes, I would." As soon as it was in his hands, he'd give the word and Lorraine and Liam and the whole Pure Bred pedigree scam would tumble down like a house of cards.

The documents looked authentic, as far as animal paperwork went. Decker had done a little research to know what to look for, and everything that was supposed to appear was there, including the seal. "Okey-dokey, Smokey, it's a wrap."

He closed the cage door and picked the carrier up. "These guys will be coming with me."

"You can't take all of them. I already have buyers lined up for the other two," Lorraine protested.

Decker heard a human squawk come from the corridor outside Lorraine's closed office door. "I'm not buying them. They aren't yours. And they aren't Bombays. They're Ottawa alley cat specials. Is there anything else you'd like to say before you're read your rights?"

There was a knock on her office door. "Come in and call the police! This man is stealing my cats."

The door opened. "I'm the police." Charlie Barr entered the room grinning. "You make this too easy, Harkness."

"I live to serve."

Decker waited for Charlie to finish reading Lorraine her rights. The kittens waited for the click of the hand-cuffs before they spun around to face the back of the room, almost shaking the cage loose from his hand as they *meeped* at the shadowed corner. "Yes, I know. We'll get you back to Joy right away, where she can scan your microchips and prove you are who I said you are."

"Is there anything else you'd like to add to your order, Harkness?" Charlie asked.

The kittens went nuts again, diving toward the corner only to bounce back when they hit the cage wall. "What is wrong with you guys?" he asked, not expecting an answer.

"*Meeeeep!*"

"Harkness?"

There was nothing else to be done here. Nothing else he needed. Everything had been tied in a big red bow.

Except.

Except for the one thing that had brought him to Pure Bred in the first place. The catalyst. The MacGuffin of a missing prototype which had set half a dozen other balls in motion.

"Give me a minute." What were the odds NPU would send an invoice to Kitten Caboodle for E.L.V.I.S. *today*? With the doll being valued at over ten thousand dollars, whoever had possession of it without a receipt was guilty of a lot more than a shoplifting misdemeanor.

"I wonder if E.L.V.I.S. has left the building," Decker said aloud.

"What?" Lorraine asked. It was the only word she'd spoken since she said, "I want my lawyer."

"I was hired to find a missing prototype for North Pole Unlimited. An E.L.V.I.S. model. I told you about it, Charlie. Lorraine is the store's manager, and she assured me it wasn't shipped to Pure Bred. Today NPU sent the invoice to Kitten Caboodle, which means if that doll is here, Lorraine is guilty of receiving stolen property."

"I am not a thief. Liam stole the cats," Lorraine insisted.

"I didn't say you stole the terrible trio. You did, however, try to sell falsely them as purebreds. But we aren't talking about that. We're talking about a twelve-inch doll with rubber shoes and a shiny utility belt worth a lot more than any cat. I bet if I took a step over there" — Decker pointed to the corner— "I'd find more of Kitten Caboodle's missing property."

In the end, he didn't take the step. His former partner took it for him. Charlie reached into the corner and pulled the doll out by its head. Decker tried not to flinch at the thought of thousands of dollars of electronics and micro-gears being squished in his friend's iron grip. Instead, he took the evidence bag Charlie dug out of his pocket, wrapped it around the doll and sealed it tight.

Two cases closed.

16. JOY

Joy clenched the lapels of her coat as she walked across the parking lot against the wind. The brisk air cleared her head of the usual daze she was in when she thought about Decker.

Since the catnapping a week and a half earlier, thinking about him was an hourly occurrence.

When Decker returned to Kitten Caboodle two hours after he'd left, with all three kittens in tow, Joy was not ashamed to say she kissed him in front of her boss, the police officers taking their statements, and mall security. She almost kissed his friend Charlie too, but managed to restrain herself to a hug when it came to him.

But first she and Rob had scanned the kittens and showed Charlie the cats were, in fact, already microchipped and registered as belonging to the shelter.

Then they had to explain what had happened with the fake coupons. Inspector Barr said it was a relatively new scam which the police had tracked back to a bunch of university students. A few days later, he reported Liam had apparently teamed up with them and used the coupon confusion as a distraction to steal the cats.

"About the second theft," the cop said after they scanned the kittens.

"Second theft?" Joy had done a head count after Decker left. All dogs, cats, birds, and guinea pigs were accounted for. She'd counted twice. The merchandise was a secondary concern, since it would take at least a day to find out how many Funsters had walked out the door.

"Are you aware North Pole Unlimited has a toy doll worth more than ten thousand dollars? It's called an E.L.V.I.S. model, I believe," Inspector Barr said.

"Yes, the one Decker was looking for. We got an invoice for it this morning," Joy said. She was about to say it had to be a mistake, but she saw Decker put a finger to his lips. She took the hint and stopped speaking.

"We found the doll in the manager's office at Pure Bred. It's likely it was stolen at the same time as the kittens, although both the manager and her accomplice are denying it. If you're willing to provide a copy of that invoice, we'll add it to the list of charges."

Behind him, Decker nodded, silently telling her to agree. He reached for Rob's arm, to give him the same advice. Rob waved him off; apparently, he didn't need the warning. The men let Joy keep talking. "I'll have to check with Rob, but I think we can do that," she said.

Truthfully, she didn't care about the doll. She had her boys back. It was enough. The police were welcome to everything else. Inspector Barr took her and Rob's statements, the coupons, and the invoice, and then he, Decker and E.L.V.I.S. left.

Decker showed up at her apartment after she got home from her shift and didn't leave her side all evening. The only exception was when Pumpkin cried for him in the kitchen until Decker went to check on him and his three little brothers.

Decker started adoption proceedings the next day.

Joy skipped his background check.

He had stiff competition. Kitten Caboodle had made the evening news, and people were clamoring to adopt the "cat-napped" kittens, as well as their other animals. The shelter had also acquired all the animals from Pure Bred after it had been shut down pending a full criminal investigation. Fortunately for them, Joy and Rob had final say on who went home with whom.

As a result of the booming sales, the fact their biggest competitor had vanished overnight, and official notification that he didn't have to pay for an eleven-thousand-dollar doll, Rob had given her a raise and a bonus.

At first, she thought it was a nice surprise that would allow her to stay at Kitten Caboodle a while longer. She hadn't heard back from the employment agency regarding her last interview anyway. The bonus was also enough to put down as a huge deposit against pet damage at an apartment building allowed cats where she put in an application. In a convenient coincidence, Decker had been hired to run her background check for the rental company.

Too bad Joy might not be around to enjoy the move.

Her luck continued to improve. A week after that, she'd received a call from the agency telling her that she'd made it to the second round of interviews. These ones were in person, in Ottawa. Thankfully, Rob had responded to her emergency email and agreed to cover the first half of her shift the next day.

She hadn't told Decker about it. She didn't want to cause unnecessary tension if she didn't get the job.

A familiar man in a golf shirt and sport coat rose from behind the table in the hotel conference room. "Hi, Joy. I'm Nick Klassen. It's nice to meet you in person," he said.

"Hi, Mr. Klassen."

"Just Nick. Please, sit."

She took a seat, and he gestured at a plate heaping with cookies, and an assortment of drinks on the table. Joy took a bottle of water, more to keep her hands busy than because she was thirsty.

"I know it's unorthodox not to know the name of the company you're applying for, especially at this stage. We've found interviews go better if we discuss exactly what you'll be doing and what your compensation will be before we talk about whom you'll be doing it for," he said. "Are you ready to get started?"

The more Nick spoke, the more excited she got. It sounded like a dream job. Working directly under a veterinarian, caring for all kinds of animals. With the salary they were offering, she could almost swing a down payment on a small house of her own if the price was right.

Then came the kicker. The company wasn't in Ottawa. It wasn't even in the province. Joy's heart dropped.

"I know this is a lot to take in. Go home, think about it. I'll contact you later this week and you can let me know what you've decided," Nick said.

Joy was fairly sure she shook his hand before she

walked out of the room. The rest was a blur until she parked in front of Decker's office.

He must have been looking out the window when she arrived, because he met her at the door. "Joy, I wasn't expecting you, but you have great timing. I have good news and bad news," Decker said. "How do you want it?"

It seemed he was having the same type of day as she was. "Me, too. Give me yours in the same order," she said.

He pulled her arm, and she tumbled onto the client sofa with him. "You passed your renter's security check—"

"Shocker," she interrupted, smiling.

Joy shut up when he mock-frowned at her. "Quiet. You passed, and if you want it, you can move in at the beginning of January. That's my good news. What's yours?"

"I've been offered a new job," she said.

"Congratulations! I didn't realize Rob was giving you a promotion too."

"He's not. It's with a new company." This was harder than she expected. "And now we're getting into my bad news, so you first," Joy said.

"I might have an even cheaper, pet-friendly place for you, if you're interested."

"I'm interested! But how is that bad news? Did somebody die in it?"

She stilled when he gave her a hug. In the last two weeks, she'd come to know his squeezes. This one told her to brace. "No. It might be vacant because we're getting to my bad news. I've been offered a job too. It's a great opportunity."

That may have been so, but if it was bad news, he didn't have to take it. "You like working for yourself. You said so." In one of their over-dinner conversations, Decker had told her being his own boss was the best part of being a private investigator, even when the money was tight.

"It wouldn't be a regular job. Well, it is, but it's for a unique company. It wouldn't be the normal nine-to-five." He huffed, like he'd made himself laugh. "Nothing about it is going to be normal. I'd be really good at it. It's not a forever deal. If I stay there for a few years, I'll be set up to reopen my agency or do whatever I want to do in the future."

It sounded good for him. A great opportunity. "Is the cheap place you found for me yours?" she asked. It was the logical progression. There weren't too many great opportunities for a private investigator in Ottawa. He was trying to tell her he was leaving.

He didn't answer in words, but his hug said yes.

"When?" Her voice cracked on the single word.

"Not until you're settled."

Joy refused to sniffle. Or let herself melt into Decker's arms. Maybe her bad news wasn't so bad after all. If she was going to be alone again, she'd better get used to handling bad news on her own. She couldn't afford to follow him, not without a job lined up. Her bonus wouldn't be enough of a cushion to rent an apartment for a few months until she got one. Not to mention, he hadn't asked her to come with him.

"Now we're back to my bad news. My new job wouldn't be here either." This was it. They were both going their separate ways.

Suddenly, Nick Klassen appeared in Decker's office door. He had a tablet in one hand and a monster-sized coffee cup in the other. "Sorry I didn't knock, but my hands were full. Hello again, Joy."

"If your hands were full, how did you open the door?" Joy asked.

"That is a very good question," he said. Then he promptly ignored it and continued speaking. "Since you're here, and talking with this gentleman, I might as well give you the final details about your job offer. It might help make your decision easier. The position we'd like to offer you is with North Pole Unlimited. We discussed salary, but I didn't mention that we also offer subsidized, pet-friendly employee housing. It's a great place to work. I think I've talked Decker into signing with us."

Joy didn't remember sitting back down on the couch. Her head spun. "You want both of us?"

"We were looking at Decker to fill our head of security position. You had already made it to the interview stage with your application before I realized you were in Ottawa as well. I had no idea you two knew each other when I arrived in town," Nick said. "Although it seems somebody did," he muttered under his breath.

"How about you give her a minute, Nick?" Decker said. His tone was almost an order, although it was laced with humor.

"Sure, I've got to get the contracts from my truck anyway. You can tell her the rest." Nick wandered back out the door, sipping his coffee.

Decker slipped his hand around her shoulders and traced circles on her back. "I never got a chance to tell you who wants me for their chief of security."

Joy felt a thousand pounds lighter. "Are you serious? Nick Klassen offered you a job too?"

"He says the company owns an apartment complex.

And have two single units available on the same floor. The cats could visit with each other."

"We have family units too," Nick shouted from the other side of the door.

"Not helping, Nick!" Decker pulled her closer. "No pressure," he said softly, "but if you're really looking for something new, and a job and apartment where you can keep the terrible trio, and want to have an adventure in the frozen tundra, because North Pole Unlimited's headquarters is just outside Winnipeg, there's really nothing keeping you in Ottawa, is there?"

"Not if you're not here."

Decker must have liked her answer. He wouldn't have kissed her like that if he didn't. She forgot everything but the kiss, which was full of sweetness and promises and warmth. She pressed her lips against his one more time, then pulled away.

"Are we taking the jobs?" he asked.

"Was there any question?"

"Well, I'm not sure if your feelings for me are as strong as the ones I have for you, so I have to ask. I'm in love with you, Joy."

"You love me?" Her jaw dropped. She knew how she felt, but it was so fast. She didn't expect him to be feeling the same way so quickly.

He laughed at her stunned expression. "I adopted a cat for you. I'm not taking it and leaving you behind. But—"

"I love you too, Decker!" she interrupted. "Whether or not you adopt Pumpkin."

He kissed her again. This time she had enough of her wits about her to realize they were right in the middle of the office with her potential future employer right outside the door. She didn't care.

"What are we going to do now? It's a great opportunity for me, but I don't know the details of your offer. If you want to take yours, I say we go. If you don't, we stay," Decker said, as if his unexpected revelation hadn't knocked her world off its axis.

"I say we go for it."

"Excellent!" Neither of them had noticed Nick open the door again. "If you'll sign these offers of employment, and this stack of nondisclosure agreements, I can tell you what North Pole Unlimited really does, and what you'll be doing there," Nick said.

Pumpkin launched himself onto the table from wherever he'd been hiding. He sniffed at the forms, then sat on his haunches and pushed them toward Decker with his nose.

Decker handed Joy a pen from his desk. "Even Pumpkin approves. You sign, I sign."

Joy hesitated on the last signature line. "What do you mean 'what you really do'? You're a toy company, right?"

Nick choked on his coffee. "Sign first."

EPILOGUE

North Pole Unlimited Headquarters
December, Manitoba, Canada

The conference table groaned under the weight of two good-bye cakes: one for his boss, George Macintyre, and the other for Constantine Phelps, NPU's retiring head of security. The security chief had agreed to stay till the end of the year to get his replacement through his first Christmas with the company, but he wanted his cake early.

Decker was going to work out fine. Locating and retrieving a malfunctioning E.L.V.I.S. prototype which had been programmed to hide was enough to earn him the job without any objections from the board. Finding it while at the same time busting an illegal purebred pet scamming organization and cracking a shoplifting ring was just showing off. He had already increased the company's internet security and presented a proposal to bring rescue animals into their manufacturing plants as guard dogs. Nick was pretty sure that idea had come from Dr. Farnsworth's new veterinary assistant.

Nick still wasn't certain how his grandmother had arranged for Decker's new girlfriend to be hired at the same time. There was no doubt Joy was a great fit, but Nick didn't know how the head of the Animal Care department had even found out about her. NPU background checks took months to complete once the decision to hire was made. They usually used a local detective to investigate applicants, but Dr. Farnsworth had somehow arranged for one out of Toronto to look into Joy's case.

He decided he wasn't going to question it too hard considering how well it had all worked out.

Dr. Andrea Farnsworth and the rest of the staff in the Animal Care department thought Joy walked on water. She didn't spend much time with the larger animals, but she reorganized and took over the puppy and kitten rooms like a boss. Anyone who got a pet from one of NPU's sponsored shelters was going to be a good pet parent. Or else. Nick smiled at the thought of her ferocity.

His grandmother sidled up next to him. "Nice party. Is this your doing?"

"No, it was all Jilly."

"She needs a raise." She handed her empty cake plate off to a wandering waitress who was collecting them and said, "Why don't you walk me back to my office?"

Whether she was asking as his grandmother or boss, the answer was the same. "Of course. What can I do for you?"

She took his arm as they walked across the freshly polished marble floor of the lobby. "I have news. John Tinder is going out on medical leave indefinitely."

"Indefinitely?"

She nodded, her eyes misty. "We don't expect him back for a long time, and when he does return, he's asked to be given a desk job. We're looking for replacement, but the person has to be willing to travel. We have someone in mind, but I think I want a field test before we officially announce him as the new senior manager in Mergers and Acquisitions. We'll talk later."

Here we go again.

THE END

RECIPE: DUTCH CINNAMON COFFEE CAKE

1 cup sour cream
1 tsp baking soda
¼ cup butter or margarine
1 cup white sugar
2 eggs, beaten
1 ½ cups flour
1 ½ tsp baking powder
1 tsp vanilla

¼ cup brown sugar and 1 tbsp cinnamon – set aside

In a separate bowl, sprinkle baking soda over sour cream and mix well. Let rest for five minutes. It will double or triple in size.

Cream butter and sugar. Add eggs, baking soda and sour cream. Add flour, baking powder, and vanilla.

Pour half the batter into a greased pan (9"x9"). Sprinkle half the cinnamon and sugar mixture over batter. Add the rest of the batter. Sprinkle the rest of the cinnamon and sugar mixture over the top.

Bake at 350F for 35 minutes.

Elle's Notes:

If using a Bundt pan, sprinkle some of the cinnamon sugar mixture in the base of the pan and add the rest to the middle.

This cake freezes wonderfully, and thaws quickly if you need to pull it out for unexpected Christmas company.

HOLLIS AND IVY

A North Pole Unlimited Romance
By
Elle Rush

BLURB

Christmas is a season of surprises, but Ivy isn't sure if Hollis is one of Santa's helpers sent to help her, or a Grinch in disguise.

Unlucky Ivy Teague can't shake the plague of bad luck following her around Whistler, BC. Business is so dire she'll have to close her flower shop unless a holiday miracle lands on her doorstep. Then he arrives.

By-the-numbers Hollis Dash is in town to finalize a business contract with Ivy's rival. It doesn't take long for him to realize that he should be making a deal with the pretty florist down the street.

When a series of suspicious events target Teague Flowers, the pair find themselves caught in a real war of the roses. Hollis can only do so much to help his business competition, and Ivy is doubtful of his intentions since Hollis and her new troubles appeared at the same time. If they can trust each other--and Christmas spirit floating through town, they might make it to the new year together.

PROLOGUE

MID-NOVEMBER
North Pole Unlimited Headquarters,
December, Manitoba, Canada (25 kilometres south-
east of Winnipeg)

His coffee had the perfect combination of hot and bitter to kick-start his brain after he'd frozen it on the drive to work. Winter had arrived, and the fluffy, ankle-high snow turned the dirty, barren landscape into a glittering, holiday wonderland. Nick Klassen, vice-president of Human Resources at North Pole Unlimited, didn't have time to appreciate the view. He was heading into a meeting that he'd spent the last week preparing for.

"Since John won't be returning to work in a travelling capacity, we need to fill the eastern senior manager position as quickly as possible. I've been through your list of candidates and know what I think. How do you feel about Hollis Dash?" his boss asked.

"I like him." Hollis was his first choice. Nick had

known the former accountant for five years. He knew the Mergers and Acquisitions department inside out and could spot a financial error at twenty paces. As far as Nick was concerned, Hollis's only flaw was his despicable ability to win every sports pool at the office. Nick was convinced they had all been fixed.

Adelaide Klassen looked thoughtful at his assessment. "His annual reviews are good, and John also provided a recommendation for him. I'm still not sure, though. I'd like to see how Hollis does in the field." The steely-haired family matriarch and company president tapped her lower lip. It looked like a thoughtful gesture, but Nick wasn't fooled. They both knew she had a plan ready to put in motion.

"Okay. We're looking at that candy shop in New Brunswick—"

"No."

"How about the game designer in Ottawa who has the escape—"

"No. I know he can investigate new businesses and bring them into the fold successfully. I'm thinking more of a struggling business under the North Pole Unlimited umbrella which may have to be cut loose."

Ending business relationships was more challenging than acquiring them. Nick mulled over the options as he stared into the blaze in the fireplace in the corner. He considered the dozens of reports that crossed his desk every week and thought of a winner. "We have an affiliate florist in Whistler, British Columbia. They've had a four-hundred-percent increase in complaints in the last six months. They've declined our offers to help, claiming their problems are due to a competitor. They say they're handling it and should show improvement in the next quarter."

"That's the one," Adelaide agreed. "I think Hollis should check them out in person in order to decide if the affiliation can be salvaged, or if NPU should terminate our contract with them. We can't have anyone damaging our reputation, even by proxy." She gave a firm nod, indicating her conviction of the company she pretended she'd allowed Nick to choose.

Nick shook his head. "I'm sorry. We were talking about filling the position in Ontario. Did you say you wanted to send Hollis in person? To Whistler?" Anyone who had spent an hour with Hollis knew he hated the mountains. His acrophobia flared if he used a step stool. Putting him on a plane and sending him into the mountains was not a good idea.

"He'll thank me for it later," Adelaide said.

Nick doubted it, but he knew the decision was made.

1. IVY

"Hi, Maggie. Hi, Captain," Ivy called out in greeting as she came through the front door of Teague Flowers and flipped the sign to Open. A blast of warm, flower-scented air enveloped her, chasing away the chill from her walk from the parking lot. November in the mountains was not for the weak of heart, but the scenery made it all worthwhile.

Whistler was surrounded by beautiful, snowcapped peaks and evergreen mountainsides. It was impossible to find a bad view unless she walked to the other end of Whistler's upper village and caught sight of Love in Bloom, her competition and nemesis. Instead, Ivy concentrated on the large bird cage in the middle of the store, admiring the yellow and green parrot within. "I hope my beautiful girl had a good night. What do pirates call their vacations?"

"Arrr."

"And?"

"Arrr," the bird repeated.

"Good girl!"

"Kisses!" the bird said. Ivy blew her a kiss, and the bird hopped from foot to foot in delight.

She pulled her heavy apron over her shirt and prepared to get to work. The cooler was full of flowers begging to be used. "Did we have any online orders waiting? I loaded my new arrangement designs onto the website over the weekend." She'd had an idea for some baby's breath and silver pinecones which would make an amazing, winter-themed centerpiece.

"Nothing."

"Anything on voice mail?"

Her assistant winced. "No orders, but there was a message. The Wicked Witch of Villa Montague has left two messages already."

"We just opened."

"Apparently, you should sleep here. Sorry to start your day with bad news, but she wants to speak to you immediately," Maggie Oh said.

It was a lie. Maggie was not sorry. She was thrilled that she wasn't the one who would have to deal with the miserable, miserly hotel manager; the little dance she did when she handed Ivy the message slips gave her away.

Ivy didn't blame her. Ellen Franks had contacted her that fall with a Christmas order: twenty dozen poinsettias, one for each room in the ski town's most expensive hotel. Teague Flowers had been trying to get into the chain hotels for years, but the branded ones had their plants and arrangements done in Vancouver and driven out. Ivy thought she'd struck gold when she got the contract.

She'd been blinded by success and desperation. Every week since, the hotel manager had called with yet another requirement to fulfill. Currently, Ivy was barely breaking even on the deal. Any more changes were going to put her in the red.

She took a moment to steel her nerves, then dialed the number which had become much too familiar over the past month. "Miss Franks, this is Ivy Teague, returning your call. What can I do for you today?"

"I need to let you know we're cancelling our order."

"Cancelling? For the poinsettias I'm supposed to deliver at the end of the week?"

"Love in Bloom contacted us and offered a better price. I've decided to go with them for our holiday decorations. You can our refund directly to me. The mailing address is on our contract."

Ivy gulped—twice—but she refused to cry. Not over Love in Bloom. "I'll look at your paperwork this afternoon."

That sounded good, and, technically, she wasn't lying. She fully intended to look at the contract. Especially the fine print at the bottom, which said she got to keep the deposit if the order was cancelled within two weeks of scheduled delivery. The deposit wouldn't cover her costs, not even by half. But it was something.

"I'm glad you're being professional about this. I thought you might cause a fuss at the last-minute change of plans. It's just business, you know," Miss Franks continued, as if her call hadn't gutted Ivy's monthly sales and chance of staying open through to the new year.

"If you can send an email confirming the order is cancelled, I'll close your file." Ivy still didn't promise a refund.

"Right away. Good luck to you, Miss Teague. Perhaps in the future, you can be more competitive cost-wise. Love in Bloom guarantees the lowest price for the highest quality."

"I'm sure they do. Good-bye, Miss Franks."

Ivy managed to hang up the phone before she exploded. "I hope all the petals fall off the day after you pay your Love in Bloom invoice."

"Problem, boss?" Maggie asked as she tied a green apron over her purple turtleneck.

"Not at all. Hey, do you know anyone who wants to buy two hundred and forty poinsettias?"

2. HOLLIS

HOLLIS DASH LOOKED out the window of his rented, white four-wheel drive and shivered as he surveyed the winter scene in front of him. A crew with a cherry picker was replacing a string of Christmas lights hanging between two lamp posts. As if the ten thousand other holiday decorations around Whistler weren't enough.

He picked up his phone and responded to his last text. *Do you know what Whistler's elevation is? The highway is a death trap.* He knew the assignment, which had forced him to make the drive up here, was a not-so-secret attempt on his life. His baseball team had made it to the World Series, and Nick's was so bad it had been swept in the division semi-finals. But that was no reason for Nick to ship him to the top of the world with no chance of escape.

The dancing monkey victory video Hollis had programmed to run every time his friend started his computer probably had something to do with his exile, as well. The joke had seemed worth it at the time. Now, not so much.

Instead of pinging to indicate he'd received another text, his cell rang. A picture of a goofy-looking, Henley-wearing giant lit up the screen. "What do you want now, Nick?" Hollis asked.

"Are you sure you weren't a dwarf in a former life? Grumpy, maybe?"

"Did you call for a reason? Do you need tips on next year's draft?"

"Very funny. I wanted to make sure you hadn't fallen off any mountains."

"I hate you. Good-bye." He cut Nick's belly-laugh off mid-guffaw.

Hollis missed his desk. And his filing cabinet. And the coffeemaker on top of his credenza. There was no reason he couldn't have completed this investigation from his office, with its nice view of the endless prairie. Unfortunately, he wanted the promotion to senior manager, so when the company president said jump on a plane, he jumped. If he proved himself in the mountains, he might get the job in the slightly hilly—but still mostly flat—east. He could do this one job.

The flower shop wasn't even open yet, and he'd already found one serious problem; they had competition on the other side of Whistler's upper village, the small, touristy shopping area. Two florists going head-to-head in a small town was one thing, but making people choose for an impulse buy when they were both within spitting distance of each other cut any business's odds by half.

The florist and owner knew he was coming. There ought to be a pile of papers, invoices, and other goodies for him to inspect as soon as he walked in the door. Hollis wasn't ready to face that yet. The two-hour time change was messing with his system. Only caffeine could straighten it out.

There were numerous chain coffee shops in the village, but Hollis preferred to try independents when he travelled. A food truck with "Coffee Run" painted on the side, set up on the street beside the main parking lot, caught his attention. It was brilliant marketing for a town built on ski slopes.

He wasn't the only one with caffeinated intentions. Sunlight was barely peeking over the mountains, and the line was trailing off after the morning rush. Hollis found himself standing next to a tall, gangly man with a red-and-white striped hat and matching sweater. A woman in a full-length wool coat fell in behind him.

The service was quick, the drinks were steaming, and the sugar was on the ledge beside the order window, next to a widemouthed jar of biscotti. Hollis took a deep whiff of his coffee before setting his cup on the counter. As he tucked his gloves in his pocket, he stepped to the side to make room for the next customer.

"Good morning. The usual?" the man in the truck asked.

"Make it a double, Joel. Thanks."

Something about the woman's voice—clear and light and a little husky—made him smile. He noticed it had the same effect on the food truck worker, who offered her a big grin. "One of those days, huh? Don't worry, Ivy. We've got you."

She directed that voice his way. "Excuse me, please." She pointed at the biscotti container, and Hollis sidled sideways two more steps. He wasn't about to come between a woman and her cookie. She grinned, and it hit him twice as hard as her voice. She was gorgeous. Her long, dark brown hair matched her eyes, and her friendly but anxious, "Yay, coffee," whisper made him laugh. A puff of wind brought the scent of spring, a reminder of it, even though winter had barely begun.

The woman used the tongs to pull a long, chocolate-topped cookie from the jar. Her next move happened too quickly to see. Her arm jerked, and he watched in amazement as the cookie went up, executed a perfect backward, double twist, and splashed down in his coffee.

Nobody spoke until she gave a horrified gasp and said, "And I'd like to buy the handsome man in the tan jacket a biscotti."

3. IVY

OF COURSE, she was a complete klutz in front of the cute guy. That's the way her life went these days. *See a handsome man, act like an idiot.* Ivy stared hard at his chest, looking for coffee splashes. The last thing she needed was to have to dry-clean his jacket.

"No, it's fine," the handsome stranger said.

This was one mess she could clean up without breaking the bank. "I'm either buying you a cookie or paying for the cookie and buying you a new coffee."

"You don't have to."

"Really, I insist. I can't believe I was so butterfingered."

"Actually, the Butterfinger bars have the peanut butter icing," Joel McCarthy interjected unhelpfully.

She spared a mock glare at the truck owner, well aware he moonlighted as an unofficial matchmaker for the local population. "You know what, Joel? You need to brighten this place up. Get it into the holiday spirit. Want to buy some poinsettias? Cheap? I'll have Maggie bring over some for you. Four? Six? Marco loves flowers." She had so many plants coming in, she'd be willing to trade some for coffee credits and free advertising. Everybody hit the Coffee Run while they were in town; Joel's word of mouth would make a dent in her supply.

"Thank you for the biscotti," the good-looking stranger said, distracting her from her potential sale. He lifted the cookie and dunked it in his cup, then gave it an experimental nibble. "Almond and chocolate?"

"Our bestseller," Joel said.

"I can see why."

While the Coffee Run initiated its newest fan into the biscotti appreciation club, Ivy paid Joel's partner and carefully stacked the coffees into the holder she'd brought along. The two treats she'd intended to buy lay diagonally between the cups. A cookie would be a good distraction from the disaster waiting for her at the store.

"Can I walk you back?"

Ivy didn't expect that. "What?"

"To the flower shop." The man reached behind her and plucked a spray of baby's breath which had been stuck to the back of her coat. "I was headed there, as well. I'm Hollis Dash."

"You were?" Her day was looking up. Since he wasn't a local, she figured he must be a tourist; they were easy to spot. Considering the population tripled during ski season, it wasn't a surprise. He ought to be wearing a toque, but it would cover his sandy brown hair, and she liked the short cut he sported. He didn't have any laugh lines around his hazel eyes, but he was still slightly older than her twenty-five years. Add in his friendliness and his manners, and he'd be welcome in her store anytime. "I'm Ivy."

"Exactly how cheap are your poinsettias? I heard you mention to…"

"Joel. Well, being as I have twenty dozen because a corporate order fell through at the last minute, I'll cut you a very good deal."

"As a complete stranger but someone who has experience with liquidation sales, may I offer a word of advice?" Hollis asked. His eyes held hers steadily, and Ivy found herself nodding in agreement.

"If you are going to put them on sale, give yourself some leeway. If people are purchasing something else, offer them even greater discount as an incentive to add one to their order. You can pass off a lot more that way."

It wasn't a bad idea but she'd have to ponder the numbers. "Thanks for the tip."

"It's my job." He stopped at the intersection, and Ivy took four more steps around the corner before she realized he was no longer with her. "Hollis?"

His face fell, and seeing that, hers matched it. "I thought you worked at Love in Bloom."

"No. Teague Flowers. I'm the owner." She should have known it was too good to be true. He was going to the enemy's shop. And now he knew she was planning a poinsettia sale. She'd ask if things could get worse, but she already knew the answer to that question. It could, and probably would.

"It was nice to meet you."

"You, too, Hollis."

Once he walked through Love in Bloom's doors, she'd likely never see him again.

4. HOLLIS

HOLLIS WAS IMPRESSED with how Love in Bloom shone. Everything looked brand new, from the plant stands to the cash desk. The glass windows gleamed, and a heavy, rose-scented perfume filled the tiny storefront. Classical music was being piped in through a pair of discreet speakers on the walls. But there was nobody there to meet him.

"Hello?"

A tiny woman with big blonde hair popped through the door that lead to the closed workspace at the back of the building. "Good morning. What can I help you find today?"

"The manager, please."

"Why, is there a problem?

It was not an auspicious start. "I'm Hollis Dash, from North Pole Unlimited. I have an appointment to see you this morning."

"I'm Annie Findlay." Her smile slipped for a second, but Hollis had caught it. She didn't want him there. He didn't blame her. Hollis could be as friendly as he liked, but when somebody like him showed up, it was because a company had done something to bring him to their door. It was like being called into the principal's office. In this scenario, he was the principal.

Love in Bloom was struggling, with a growing number of complaints and lackluster sales. As a partner to North Pole Unlimited, they filled all of NPU's orders in the area and, in return, received advertising on North Pole Unlimited's website and with other affiliates, as well as other benefits. But the contract had conditions.

Annie had already received one notice from NPU's corporate office asking if there were any problems their business specialists could assist with. The offer was made in good faith to all companies under the corporate umbrella if a flag went up, but once made, NPU expected to see improvements. Annie had turned them down and continued to let the store's reputation slide. The situation had to be resolved to North Pole Unlimited's satisfaction —one way or another. An in-person meeting was her last shot at redemption.

"Of course. I've been expecting you." She tried to smile bigger at him. It was a little scary.

"I'm not the boogeyman, I promise. I'm here to help. Why don't you tell me a little more about the store? You recently bought it, right?" If this was simply a matter of a new business owner being in over her head, he could be home tomorrow.

"A year ago. I worked for Mr. Iverson for a year, then bought him out when he retired. I understand why you're here—because of Teague Flowers." Her eyes narrowed, and her smile faded.

"Teague Flowers? The other florist in the village?" There couldn't be two of them.

"Ivy Teague, in particular. Ever since I took over the business, she's been out to get me. It's been horrible."

"What has she done?" If a food fight was involved, he'd believe it.

"Nothing I can prove. It's all been dirty tricks, and I know how to handle those. It's not like Ivy and her store are real competition. She'll be gone soon enough." Annie waved her hand dismissively. "But enough about that. You're here to do the audit. I have all the information you requested in the back if you'd like to get started."

Stepping into the rear half of the shop was like arriving on a different planet. Buckets of flowers sat on rickety tables, their beauty a stunning contrast to the dingy walls and scuffed floor. A dirty sink with mildewed caulking dripped in the corner. There was an office in the corner. Through the open door, Hollis saw a brand-new laptop and printer on the desktop and a television mounted on the wall. A second, empty desk mirrored it.

He, however, would be working on a folding card table set up beside the back door. A box of loose receipts sat on one side; a second box of sorted, filed papers was on the other. Annie had also provided a power bar to support any electronics he'd brought along. It was almost like she was trying to rush him out the door. While he was getting organized, she brought him a cup of steaming hot coffee and asked if he wanted her extra croissant.

Hollis recognized "get lost" when he saw it, no matter how prettily it was dressed. Luckily, he didn't scare easily. Still, he appreciated the food, so he thanked her before she ducked into her office to answer her ringing desk phone.

It took him a few minutes to get sorted, but he dove in before his coffee was cold. He debated pulling out his earbuds so he could tune out the symphony in the back-ground, but he wanted to finish listening to Annie's call first. She couldn't be expecting privacy, not with her door open and her voice on full volume. She was arguing about her dire need for twenty dozen poinsettias at the last minute.

Now he knew what had happened to Ivy's corporate order. Scooping a competitor was a time-honored tradi-tion, but generally, the second player was certain they could fulfill the order. If they didn't, they burned their reputation and ensured the competition they scooped would turn a better profit the next time. If Annie was scrambling now, it had been poor planning on her part. But it wasn't his problem.

By the time Hollis's stomach ordered him to feed it, he was thoroughly confused. He flexed his hand. His calculator finger was itchy. Maybe it was the fact every-thing was too perfect. The same bills showed up each month, almost identical in amount. No business was that consistent, especially one based on special occasions and holidays. Annie had switched suppliers since she'd taken over the store, but unless she was deliberately getting lower quality flowers and paying the same price for them, Hollis couldn't see a reason for the rise in the number of complaints she'd been receiving. There had to be some-thing to find. After lunch.

There was no shortage of places to eat in Whistler; the village had an amazing selection of restaurants that ran the gamut from tapas to pasta. He promised his stomach he'd pick one right after he scoped out the competition. He spotted Ivy through her shop window and pushed open the door.

Her head was cocked to the side as she studied a

display in the corner: a multi-tiered stand with each level containing an increasing number of poinsettias than the one above it. Ivy had alternated red and white rows. The final result was a stunning candy-cane striped Christmas tree made of flowers.

While Love in Bloom was shiny and new, Teague Flowers was lived in—not dirty or worn-out, but well-loved—furnished with freshly painted, solid wood pieces. No chrome to blind customers, just a rainbow of lively colors. It smelled truly green rather than like air freshener. It was an important distinction to his nose.

The massive bird cage in the center of the store floor was a surprise, as was the green and yellow parrot, which gave the place a tropical feel. At the moment, the bird's head was bobbing along to a song on the oldies station the two women behind the counter were listening to; it might have been Elvis, but Hollis wasn't sure.

"Hi, I'm Maggie. Can I help you?" the one who wasn't Ivy asked. She was pretty, slightly older than Ivy with short black hair and black eyes.

"Hollis, hi. What are you doing here?" Ivy asked when she looked up from her phone. "I mean... Can I help you with something?"

"Yes, but first I have to know about the bird." It made no sense to have a tropical bird in a ski resort town. When he took a closer look, he noticed one of the bird's wings was badly misshapen, like it had been broken and poorly reset, but the bird hopped around so much it was hard to tell.

"Captain? My grandmother saved her from a pet store in the eighties. Her wing was broken, so they couldn't sell her. They going to euthanize her, so Grandma brought her home. Then, when my mom moved the store from Vancouver to Whistler in the nineties, we brought her with us. She's our store mascot."

"Captain? Like Captain Jack Sparrow?"

"No, like Captain Jackie Parrot. The other guy came later and is a pale imitation to our wondrous leader. The captain is a genius. Want me to prove it?"

He was still stuck on Captain Jackie Parrot. "Sure."

"What letter comes after Q, Captain?"

"Arrrr."

"Good girl."

"Kisses!"

Ivy blew the bird a raspberry. "Isn't she amazing? But you didn't come here for a comedy show. What can I do for you?"

"Your biscotti choice this morning was excellent. I was hoping you'd have a recommendation for lunch." He wanted a chance to hear about Love in Bloom from the competition's point of view. It would be even better if he could think of a way to do it over a meal. Someplace far away from bad puns.

She checked the clock. "Wow, it's after noon. I should get something, too. How do you feel about soup and sour-dough? El Furny has knock-your-socks-off roasted red pepper soup."

He could do that. Especially with someone who might have answers for him. "May I join you?"

Hollis didn't miss the elbow she took to the ribs from her co-worker before she said, "Ow, yes, sure. Maggie can watch the shop."

She snagged her coat from the hook behind the counter and stepped around to join him. This time, instead of baby's breath, a sprig of spruce was stuck to her sleeve.

"Will you bring me back soup?" Maggie asked.

"Do you deserve soup?"

"No, but you'll bring me some anyway because you're a great boss."

Hollis enjoyed the interplay. The whole tone of Teague Flowers made it a happy place to be. Love in Bloom had felt like a library or a museum.

"Fine. I'll be back in half an hour. Don't do anything I wouldn't do."

5. IVY

SHE LED them on a brisk walk to the restaurant. Although it was only around the corner, the air quickly chilled them. Ivy was used to the damp winters, but she had no idea how her lunch date was faring. "Are you doing okay, Hollis?"

He nodded, his nose buried in a navy, knit scarf. "Yep."

"Not too cold?"

"I'm from Winnipeg," he said like it was an explanation. To an extent, it was. Winnipeg was internationally known for its inhospitable winters. But mountain cold was different than prairie cold. The humidity penetrated to the bone, no matter how many layers a person wore.

"Welcome to the coast."

They smelled the restaurant before they entered it. A cloud of spicy, meaty temptation hit them at the door. Hollis inhaled and grinned, and his smile was just as amazing as she remembered. She couldn't wait till he tried the food.

They lucked out and found a tiny bar table and two stools against the window. They were silent for the first taste, enjoying the flavors of the hot soup, but they started talking as they waited for it cool a bit.

"I'm glad you stopped in. I wanted to thank you for your advice. I took it and ran with it. Five poinsettias gone. Only two-hundred and thirty-five to go." She was working on some other ideas, but she wasn't willing to share them with him.

"That's a good start for four hours."

"Does this count as you scoping out your business rival? Annie and I generally stick to peeking in each other's windows." Teague Flowers had been going head-to-head with Love in Bloom since the nineties, when her mother had moved her grandmother's flower shop from Vancouver to the mountains. The business had always done well, even with the competition.

After her mother passed away two years earlier, Ivy inherited the shop she'd worked in her whole life. Annie Findlay had come up from Vancouver about the same time, working as an assistant to Love in Bloom's owner, Mr. Iverson. The old man had retired to Victoria the previous winter, selling the business to Annie. That was when the two florists' friendly rivalry had turned into something less fun, and Ivy's green world had turned to black. Every time she'd thought she was catching a break, it had either gone bad or Annie had caught a bigger one. In less than a year, Teague Flowers had gone from successful and profitable to floundering and barely breaking even.

Ivy raised her chin and squared her shoulders. *Shake it off*. She was responsible for Teague Flowers. Nobody else. Sure, she was struggling at the moment—more so now that she had a forest of white and red poinsettias in the back room—but she could handle it. All she needed was a little bit of Christmas luck. The disastrous flukes she'd been experiencing couldn't last forever.

Meeting Hollis was a bit of good luck. He seemed like a nice guy—was a fun lunch date, liked soup, had horrible taste in florists. But nobody was perfect.

"No, not at all. I don't actually work for Love in Bloom. They're an affiliate to my company, North Pole Unlimited. We like to check on all our contractors, so here I am. In the clouds. High, high above sea level. Where you can die by falling off a mountain." The last bit was said with a grumble.

"Does that mean you won't be going up the mountain to check out the view? Maybe take a ride up the Sea-to-Sky gondola down in Squamish?" The popular tourist attraction transported people up the side of the mountain and offered them a breathtaking look at Howe Sound. Of course, it also nearly vertical in places, which would probably not appeal to someone who was afraid of heights.

"Do I look like I have a death wish? No." He laughed, but his grip on his spoon was white-knuckled.

"You are *really* from Winnipeg."

"Yes, I'm totally a prairie boy—where everything is flat and not trying to kill you."

She laughed. It wasn't an uncommon reaction for a visitor, but Ivy didn't understand it at all. How could anyone not fall in love with the mountains?

"Does your company send you out to a lot of businesses?"

"Not so far, but I'm applying for a new position where I'll be doing it a lot. I don't mind. I like travelling." He wiped his bread crust around the bowl, sopping up the last of his soup, and popped it into his mouth. "I liked your poinsettia tree. It reminded me of my niece's school fundraiser. They had a similar one last year for"—Hollis scratched his head—"band, maybe. She always has something going on."

A lightbulb went off over Ivy's head. He'd just given her a fantastic idea. She had a sneaking suspicion he'd done it on purpose. Hollis had gone silent for a full minute after he said it, as if giving her brain time to formulate the plan it had. She didn't care; if it had been on purpose, it was the second time he'd helped her that day, and she'd be forever grateful. If it had been an innocent comment, and she'd been inspired all on her own, it was still a good idea.

"You said an order was cancelled," Hollis said, keeping his eyes on his bowl.

"Yes. Love in Bloom picked it up. But you already knew that." The goodwill she'd felt began to evaporate.

"Are they serious competition?"

"In a town this big, anything is serious competition." She wasn't going to admit to a stranger how much she was hurting.

"I suppose that's true enough." He leaned back and let a waitress clear their dishes. "Excellent soup suggestion, Ivy. Thanks for coming with me. I enjoy travelling but eating alone gets old."

"I can imagine."

They went their separate ways, but her good mood grew when Maggie greeted her with a thumbs-up. "One more poinsettia down." Ivy didn't know what she'd do without Maggie.

Her friend was the oldest daughter of Hong Kong immigrants who had come to Vancouver in the late nineties. Maggie liked to say she'd come to Whistler to ski for the weekend after her final university exams and had forgotten to go home. She began working part-time at the flower shop to supplement her waitressing income during the slow season while Ivy's mother, Lily, was still running the store. After Ivy's mom had passed away, Maggie stopped waitressing and started at Teague Flowers full-time. She'd been a godsend, and all Ivy had to do to keep her happy was look the other way on mornings when there was fresh powder on the slopes.

"Excellent! I have a plan to get rid of some of them in bulk. Can you mind the front of the store while I make some calls from the office?" Ivy wanted to get started immediately. She didn't know if her sales pitch was viable. All she knew was she had a very small window in which to move a large number of plants.

Two hours later, the soup had worn off, her throat was parched, and she'd sold two dozen poinsettias to a daycare center at a discount for them to resell at full price. The daycare director loved the idea; she'd said it was better than chocolates sale they'd been thinking of doing in the new year.

Ivy's good mood grew when her phone rang again. The call display showed Villa Montague, and she knew exactly who was calling and why.

"What do you mean, you're keeping my deposit?" Ellen Franks shouted through the phone.

"It was in your contract. If you cancel within two weeks of the delivery date—which you confirmed with me in numerous emails—I am authorized to keep your deposit. I've already taken receipt of the flowers. If you'd like to reinstate your order, I'd be happy to discuss that."

"This is robbery."

Ivy flinched at the insult. She wasn't deliberately trying to cause problems, but she had a business to run too. "It was in the contact, Ms. Franks. You agreed to it."

The hotel manager huffed loudly, then hung up in her ear.

6. HOLLIS

HOLLIS FOUND North Pole Unlimited hadn't skimped on accommodations. They'd booked him into Villa Montague. The manager had checked him in personally, and Miss Franks had told him to call her direct line if he needed anything. His hotel bed was like sleeping on a cloud. Despite the comfort, he awoke early—very early, considering the time change—and decided a walk around the upper village would be a good way to work up an appetite.

The massive amount of overnight accumulation had been predicted but had arrived silently. The hush of the morning was slowly being broken by snow clearing equipment and people making their way to work in anticipation of the skiers and snowboarders who would soon follow. He stopped in the middle of the walkway, admiring the way the street and path lights made strange shadows on the fresh drifts. Dawn wouldn't come for another hour.

There was still enough light to see the graffiti covering the front of Teague Flowers. *Going Out of Business. Loser*. The storefront was a mess. Hollis had no idea how such vandalism had been possible with the heavy security and police presence in the area, but he supposed the thickly falling snow and starless, moonless sky had provided a lot of cover.

His sharp ears picked up a distant gasp. Hollis turned around to see Ivy standing shock-still, hands over her mouth, eyes locked on her store in horror.

His mission in Whistler wasn't to help Ivy, but he hated a bully. First, she'd lost a major contract—to the person he was supposed to be helping, no less—which would be a blow to her reputation but was part of doing business. Now her store had been attacked. Annie's words echoed in his ears. *Dirty tricks. She'll be gone soon enough.* Hollis didn't believe in coincidence, not with the literal writing on the wall. Even if Ivy was responsible for Love in Bloom's problems, revenge was not part of North Pole Unlimited's playbook.

He took another look at Ivy. She appeared to be too shocked to cry. "Ivy, are you breathing?"

She shook her head.

Hollis ducked down until he was even with her and caught her eyes. "I need you to take a breath."

She shook it again. "If I breathe—if I move—I'm going to burst into tears." She didn't realize they'd already started. Hollis watched helplessly as Ivy's face crumpled in slow motion.

He'd do anything to stop a crying woman's tears, even if he had just met her. He wrapped his arms around Ivy's trembling shoulders. She held herself stiffly, rejecting the comfort he offered—until he spoke. "This is all fixable, Ivy," he whispered in her ear.

She lost it. "I am so screwed!" she wailed. She collapsed against his chest and sobbed—for about thirty seconds. In the time it took him to blink, she pulled away and scrubbed her eyes with a tissue she'd retrieved from her coat pocket.

"I'm just one disaster after another these days, aren't I?" she said, trying for a laugh.

"I bet you've had better weeks." His quip almost got a smile. He wanted one.

Ivy gestured at her defaced building. "Not lately. This is going to take hundreds, if not thousands, of dollars to clean. My insurance is already giving me a hard time about another claim I made for broken windows over the summer. I'll have to pay for this out of pocket and pray they reimburse me."

That didn't work for him. Neither did her being so upset. "Here's something you wouldn't know about me. Guess what I did as a summer job to put myself through college?"

"Were you a magician?" Her voice was half humor-ous, half hopeful.

"I did historical home renovations. I have a ton of experience with paint and paint removal." Hollis was lying through his teeth. He'd painted his cousin's rundown—thus, historical—summer cottage. Once. Well, he'd helped. He wasn't great at keeping his brush in the designated areas, but this was paint removal. It had to be easier.

Her grateful smile rocked him. Her coffee brown eyes held a spark he hadn't seen before. The color flushing her cheeks made her look alive instead of the near-death shade she'd been moments before. "Are you kidding me?" she demanded.

For a second, he was so overcome by the look on her face, he couldn't remember what she was asking about.

Cleaning up the vandalism, right. "Yes. I mean— No, I'm not kidding. Yes, I can fix this." A little turpentine, a little scrubbing, a little North Pole Unlimited proprietary formula for paint removal, and he'd have the storefront looking better than new. A strange look crossed Ivy's face, and it quickly turned to panic. She'd barely admitted she had a problem with her poinsettias. She wasn't going to ask for help now. "I can't ask you to do that. You're working."

"I can set my own schedule while I'm in Whistler, as long as I get the job done. Give me till lunch," he suggested. "If I haven't made enough progress to impress you by then, you can fire me."

"You don't work for me."

"Then you don't have anything to lose, do you?" he argued.

Ivy gulped. "Are you sure? I could use a hand."

"Is there a hardware store in Whistler?" He figured there had to be something close. With the number of tourists and related businesses, people couldn't wait to make repairs—not even the couple hours it would take to drive something up from Vancouver.

"Yes."

"I walked over from the hotel. Since you drove, why don't you head there now. I'll get a closer look at this mess, then text you a list beyond the standard turpentine, scrub brushes, and rags."

As soon as she left, he pulled out his phone, not wasting a second. He spent ten minutes on the phone begging Jilly Lewis, Nick's executive assistant, to email him the company's top-secret cleaning formula. He knew the Research and Development chemistry team had invented something to help out the R&D design team after one too many exploding potion incidents. After Jilly finally came through with a list of commercially available products to mix to get an equivalent to their workshop's guaranteed paint remover, Hollis texted them to Ivy. Fortunately, she replied to say all the ingredients were readily available.

The sun was up by the time Ivy returned and he had the mixture ready for use. The upper village was coming to life, including a stroller-pushing young mother, who gasped at the sight.

"What a rotten mess. Isn't it terrible?" Hollis asked as he squirted fresh turpentine on a squiggle covering the signage above the door. He was grateful Ivy thought to purchase spray bottles. They allowed him to keep one hand on the stepladder.

"It's horrible," the woman agreed.

"I'm going to have paint thinner fumes in my nose for a week. Thankfully, I can go inside for some fresh air," Hollis said. *Come on, take the bait.*

His comment drew her attention from the vandalism to him. "Oh, is the flower shop still open?"

"Absolutely. They have some wonderful poinsettias available."

Hollis could tell the moment the decision had been made. Her smile deepened, and her baby girl gurgled at seeing her mommy happy. "We're visiting my mom. She loves flowers. I bet she'd love some on the dining room table," the woman said.

Hollis climbed down the ladder, set his scrub brush on the window ledge, and held the door open for her. She wheeled her stroller into the store, and Hollis mentally added one to Ivy's "Poinsettia Sales" column.

After she left, he carefully spritzed Jilly's mixture on

the section he'd soaked with turpentine. An entire section of spray paint bubbled away from the bricks and took years of soot and ground-in dirt with it. He grinned when he rinsed off the area. When he'd finished cleaning, the storefront looked better than new. Ivy was up to her elbows in a flower delivery when he went to tell her he was done, so he left without a word.

He'd see her again. It was a small town.

It was smaller than he thought. By the time he returned to his hotel to change and walked back to Love in Bloom, Annie already knew about it. "I thought you were in town to analyze my business, not help my competition," Annie said. "Ivy probably did it to herself for sympathy. She'd do anything to drum up business. Did she say I was responsible?"

He didn't have to justify his actions, but he wanted Annie to know where he stood. "No, she didn't. And by helping her, I was helping you. Some people might have looked your way considering what was written. "Going Out of Business" points a circumstantial finger at the competition, which, in this case, is you." Her comments had his brain spinning. Why would Annie's first assumption be that Ivy would accuse her? Was it a guilty conscience?

"Do you think I'd do that?"

The thought had crossed his mind briefly, but he'd never make an accusation without proof. "I don't think you'd be so obvious and clumsy to do something like vandalism." Now that he'd discovered the animosity between Whistler's two florists was mutual, he had to look at the possibility Ivy truly was behind the complaints against Love in Bloom—but he didn't want to. "You looked pleased when I came in. Good news?"

"I sourced the poinsettias I needed. It's a great oppor-tunity since the larger hotels in the area have their own suppliers. The independents are easier to break into. Teague Flowers used to have a monopoly, but they've been losing customers. I picked up their fall mum order from a bed-and-breakfast collective earlier this fall. If Ivy can't compete, I'll happily step into the void. She can't match my prices anyway. Ivy has been losing ground ever since her mother died. It would probably be better for her to close her doors and move away to get a fresh start."

Losing the fall flowers had to have been another blow for Ivy. In Hollis's experience, there were only two reasons someone switched vendors: poor quality or better prices. He'd seen Ivy's shop, so the first didn't seem to be a problem. The second would show in Love in Bloom's books. He made a mental note to look for it; now he was curious.

INTERLUDE

North Pole Unlimited Headquarters

"Okay, Hollis, you're on speaker. How's it going at the top of the world?" Nick Klassen asked, much to the amusement of the women listening in. The office had a pool of how long Hollis would survive in Whistler before demanding they bring him home. Nick had already lost his chance, having put his money at the twelve-hour mark. Jilly, however, was still in the running as long as Hollis lasted past the three-day mark. He was two days in.

"Are we alone or am I on speaker?"

"My grandmother is here with me." His office was smaller, but this way, he didn't have to drag all his files around the building. His assistant had broken out the good cookies as soon as she heard Adelaide would be joining them.

"In that case, everything is going swimmingly and I'm not freaking out at the elevation all the time at all," Hollis said with a laugh. "Are you ready for my report?"

"Are you finished already?" Adelaide Klassen asked. Nick knew his buddy was good, but he hadn't thought he was that good.

"I wish."

"Was it worth the trip?"

"My acrophobia says no. But for the company, yes. We have a serious issue here," Hollis reported. "Annie Findlay, the owner, is denying she's having any problems. She insists that all the customer complaints are fake and were instigated by her competition in Whistler."

"It wouldn't be the first time," Nick said. Internet review sites and comment pages could be a cesspool, even for something like a flower shop. "What's your impression of Love in Bloom?"

"I'm not seeing any problems on-site. Except for her books. They're perfect."

Nick must have misheard. Usually, his auditors complained about a company's accounts being a mess or missing altogether. "Why is that a problem?"

"Have you ever once seen a company with perfect books? I haven't. I'm spending most of my time organizing receipts, but absolutely everything has a balanced, matching entry. It gives me the creeps."

"Perhaps Miss Findlay is simply well-organized," Adelaide suggested.

"How often have you known a company to order two dozen of something and have that exact number of sales every two months for five months running?" Hollis asked. "Nobody is that good."

"Have you found anything verifiable? Or do you want to come home?" Nick asked. He trusted Hollis's judgement. They'd seen all kinds of scams over the years, some

of which were truly inspiring. But the bloodhound auditors in Mergers and Acquisitions eventually sniffed them
out. It was why North Pole Unlimited paid so much to
hire the best accountants money could buy.

"Not yet, but I want to stay. I suspect I'll find something if I dig deeper."

Nick's grandmother looked smug, which did not bode
well for Hollis. "Jilly said something about our cleaning
compound. What's that about?" she asked.

"Ivy's store was vandalized. I was helping clean her
sign and needed something that takes paint off easily. She
doesn't know what I used, so your secret formula is still
secret."

"Who's Ivy?" Nick asked.

"Ivy Teague of Teague Flowers. Love in Bloom's
competition. Both stores have been in Whistler for years,
but Ivy is struggling right now. I don't believe it's all
natural selection. I've seen how she operates. She's smart
and talented and innovative. I think someone is helping
her fail. If it's Annie Findlay at Love in Bloom, we need to
know. We don't want anyone muddying up our brand."

"Definitely not," Adelaide agreed. "You stay there as
long as you need and get to the bottom of this. North Pole
Unlimited's reputation is everything. We can't afford to
have a bad apple in our business barrel. I want answers,
Mr. Dash."

"Yes, ma'am. I'll send my next report when I have
news. I'll call anyway in a couple days if I don't," Hollis
promised before he ended the call.

Nick reclined in the leather chair his predecessor had
left behind. "We could be in big trouble here. Did you
hear what he said?" he asked his assistant.

Jilly's eyes crinkled, which made her looked like she wanted to laugh. "Yeah. I heard exactly what he said," she replied. She only lasted a second before she and Adelaide burst into giggles.

Nick got the impression he'd missed something important.

7. IVY

HER WEEK HAD PUT her through more ups and downs than the ski lifts she could see from her store windows, and Ivy was more than ready for her weekend. Ivy shut down the shop at six on Saturday, which left her an hour to prepare for a night of epic proportions.

She might be exaggerating a little, but her annual Leg-Breaker party had quickly become one of Whistler's unofficial declarations of winter's arrival. Before the ski season got into full swing, the winter tourists invaded, and the slopes became a gambler's paradise of who would make it down the black runs intact, the locals had a final pre-holiday hurrah. Ivy hosted other shop owners and permanent hotel staff in a night of early Christmas celebration, since they would not be able to gather on the actual night.

Ivy hadn't finished decorating yet. With the number of American tourists who came up for the first ski of the season over their Thanksgiving weekend, she still had a few fall decorations around the store, in contrast to the exterior, which had been Santa-ready since the day after Hallowe'en. The last of her Thanksgiving orders had gone out that day, leaving her lots of blank space on tables and shelves to be filled with glasses and food that night. She'd drag herself in the next day to clean up and finish decorating the shop for the third busiest time of year.

"Ivy, where can I put these?" Maggie came through the back door carrying a large circular platter covered with tinfoil. She was wearing a hideous, green, knit top with colored balls, which were supposed to resemble Christmas lights. The sweater was as much a tradition as the goodies on the tray—if it contained what Ivy hoped it did.

"Is that what I think it is?"

"If you're thinking iced sugar cookies, you're wrong. If you're thinking coconut Christmas trees in three flavors, you're right," Maggie teased.

"I love being right."

"No sampling beforehand."

"But I'm your boss."

"The tinfoil doesn't come off until after the first guests arrive. I don't want to be asked why I only brought half a tray of cookies. Again."

"One time!" She'd found an unguarded plate of coconut and chocolate with a delicious icing holding it all together. The grumbles she'd received from Maggie and the other partygoers had been totally worth it. The sugar high had lasted all weekend.

"No sampling."

Ivy heroically resisted temptation until the party started, mostly because Maggie kept her busy on the other side of the shop. The store was half full before Maggie came to her with a peace offering and said, "By the way, I invited that Hollis guy as a thank you for cleaning off all the graffiti."

Hollis. The graffiti. For a couple minutes, Ivy had managed to forget about her latest disaster. She'd kept an eye open for Hollis at both the Coffee Run in the mornings and in the shop over the lunch hours, but she hadn't seen him since the day he scrubbed her storefront and made it sparkle. She still hadn't said thank you. "When did you see him?"

"He stopped by this afternoon. I forgot to tell you. But he said he'd show sometime tonight."

Ivy was glad she'd worn her nice Christmas sweater instead of her goofy red one that matched Maggie's. It hugged her curves nicely, and the metallic threads sparkled when she stood beside the row of twinkling lights she'd wrapped around the poinsettia display. That was all she'd had time to put up. The back room was stuffed with plastic tote boxes full of Christmas decorations she hadn't looked through yet.

People came and went, but Ivy knew the second Hollis entered the store. Some of it was because he was a stranger, and this was a private party. But another part of her brain thought she, and everyone around him, might be responding to the kind, cheerful vibes he gave off.

She doubted he'd brought his reindeer-face tie with him on a business trip, which meant he'd taken the time to go shopping specifically for her party. And he'd stopped at his hotel for a fresh shave. The care he'd taken to look good at her party gave her a warm feeling that had nothing to do with the powerful rum ball she'd just popped into her mouth.

He'd evidently made a few friends; Marco Watson laughed when Hollis snagged a glass of eggnog with one hand and wrapped the other around Marco's arm before a pair of tipsy guests knocked the coffee truck owner into the poinsettia display. Maggie made a special trip across the crowded floor to make sure Hollis got one of her coconut Christmas to thank him for all his earlier hard work. Ivy was pleased to see he recognized the gesture for what it was, because Maggie rationed those treats like they were gold.

It was a fair comparison.

She needed a big gulp of liquid courage before she made her way over to say hello. In the past few days, Hollis had become her own knight in shining armor. It was impossible to properly thank a person for that.

"The front of the store looks amazing. You snuck away before I could thank you. So, thank you."

"It was nothing."

She stared at him hard. "You were outside, in the cold, for over two hours, scouring brick with a wire brush. Now it looks like nothing ever happened. Believe me, it was something. Let me say thank you." He had been so incredibly kind. She felt slightly guilty for not helping, but he'd told her to go inside and work. Who was she to argue with a knight?

"I was happy to help."

"Did it cause any problems with your job? I know you're supposed to be working with Love in Bloom." He could come over anytime he wanted, as far as Ivy was concerned, but not if he got in trouble for it.

"Love in Bloom takes up a lot of my time, but as I said, my schedule is flexible. I can do what I want when I'm not working. Like—"

"Kisses!" Captain yelled.

They both turned to look at the bird. "Kisses!" it repeated.

Ivy burst into laughter. She knew what was up. Every

year, they hung a sprig of mistletoe in the center of the store, right in front of Captain's cage. Somehow, she and Hollis had been jostled into position. Captain was just doing her job.

"You have to," Maggie insisted from the makeshift bar.

"If you don't, it's seven years of bad luck," Joel added.

"Dude, that's breaking a mirror."

"Do you want to risk it? Don't anger the big red man."

She blushed at the thought of trying to explain why they'd been called out. Instead of trying to find the words, she pointed straight up.

"Well, I wouldn't want to anger the big red man," Hollis said.

Ivy braced. She hadn't received a mistletoe kiss in years. Hollis cupped her chin carefully, tilted her face up to his, and placed a gentle kiss on her lips. She swore there were sparks.

Then she jumped out of his arms.

"What's wrong? Are you okay? Did I do something?"

"No, no, you were great." Her luck was still holding. Her klutzy-action-hot-guy proximity reflex was working fine. "My phone is set to vibrate. It went off in my back pocket and scared me."

"Saved by the cell."

Ivy didn't want to be saved. She pulled out her phone and saw a number that made her blink. "I'm sorry. I have to take this. It's a supplier, and I have no idea why they'd be calling me at this hour on a Saturday night." One thing was certain—it wouldn't be good news.

She skirted the boxes in her tiny office and closed the door as best she could. "Hello? This is Ivy."

"Hi, Ivy. It's Brian Applebaum from Imprint Glassworks in Vancouver. Sorry to bother you on the weekend, but 'tis the season, you know."

"Hi, Brian. How can I help you?"

"I'm calling to apologize. We've hired new Accounts Payable and Accounts Receivable people, and the departmental changes are still shaking out. I've been reviewing the last two weeks' paperwork and realized you were never sent confirmation regarding your cancellation of your holiday-themed order. Our Accounts Payable accidentally sent you an invoice, but I wanted to call to let you know to disregard it. We will be sending written confirmation next week."

"Wait, what?" Ivy knew exactly what he was talking about. She'd ordered an assortment of vases, pots, and arrangement containers for upcoming holiday orders and had chosen each design with care. She preferred to get ones which could be reused or set out for another purpose in following years. They were great, unofficial advertising for Teague Flowers. People took them out each holiday season and remembered where they'd received it from. She rifled through her overflowing inbox tray looking for the order printout she'd made for her tax receipt file.

"I was sorry to see it," Brian said. "We've enjoyed our business relationship with Teague Flowers over the years."

"And I was hoping it would continue for many more," Ivy agreed. "I have no idea what you're talking about."

"We got a fax from you, cancelling the order. Fortunately, you have great taste. It wasn't a problem to resell the stock."

She landed hard in her desk chair, dropping more than sitting. "You sold my vases?" She needed those. She had orders starting on Monday, when the shipment had been due to be delivered.

"You cancelled the order."

"By fax?" *Who used faxes anymore?* Ivy did everything online, like every other business in the twenty-first century.

She heard rustling at the other end of the line. "I was surprised, too. An actual paper fax. I didn't know our printer was still set up to receive them. It says it was sent from the Whistler Business Center. It has Teague Flower letterhead."

She couldn't wrap her head around the facts. The fax. She'd never sent anything like that. She hadn't been to the business center in months. But after ten years of using Imprint Glassworks without a problem, she believed Brian. "I don't know what you got, but I never cancelled my order. Can you please send me a copy?" Ivy needed to see for herself. If there were tangible evidence someone had faked her letterhead, she would have to view her random bad luck of late in a new light.

"I'll send it now. Are you saying it's not from you?" Brian asked.

"Definitely not. I'll happily figure out who did later. Right now, I'm more concerned about my order. Can you refill it and get it to me this week? I might have a few vases left over from last year, but I need that shipment." She was going to have to brave the bowels of her storage unit to see what was left from the previous holiday season. She hadn't been past the first couple rows of boxes since her mother died. Ivy would have to check the house, too, and hope something was stored in the garage rafters. It would be a dirty, potentially fruitless job she didn't have time for.

"I'm sorry, Ivy. Like I said, you have good taste. The products you picked sold out fast. We have some left, but there aren't a lot of options," Brian apologized.

She could guess—generic vases with no character. If she was stuck with those, her clients would be less than impressed, which would affect future orders. Whoever had cancelled her order had manage to do double damage to her business.

"Can you send me links to what you do have?" Maybe she could work with them. Dress them up somehow. She had a hot glue gun and sparkles and knew how to use them.

"I'll send you all available links in an email. Again, I'm sorry we didn't catch this earlier. I would have called to verify the cancellation, and we could have cut this off at the pass."

"Can you note in my file that I will never cancel except by email with a confirming phone call to make sure this never happens again?" Her computer pinged, and she opened the email immediately. Two clicks later she was staring at an image of the fax and, as he'd said, it appeared to be on Teague Flowers stationary. It was a copy of a copy, but it looked legitimate. Ivy was stumped. She hadn't known the business center had a fax machine. She'd never opened an account there.

"I'll make that note now. Anyway, I'll let you go. I'll send you an updated list of links on Monday. Enjoy the rest of your weekend."

"You, too, Brian."

She didn't know how long she sat there staring at the paper she'd printed. Annie had managed to scoop her fall contract with the local bed-and-breakfast group, which had hurt, but her business plan took stuff like that into account. The Villa Montague order was never going to make her much money in the first year; she was using it to get a foot in the door, and it had ended up crushing her toes. Now her entire Christmas season was in jeopardy. And she had no idea how to fix any of it.

She heard a faint knock, and her door swung inward. Hollis stood there with two cups of cranberry red punch in his hands. "Are you coming back to the party?"

She had guests. She couldn't hide. "Absolutely."

He was beside her in an instant. "What's that?"

Ivy flipped the paper facedown and placed it on her desk. "Work, and tonight is supposed to be about play. Is that for me?"

"Yes. I came in here for two reasons—three, actually." He handed her one of the cups. "Here's some punch. Maggie said you asked for a glass. Joel wanted me to warn you Marco is singing the alphabet song to Captain and keeps starting over at "S". The bird looks like it's getting annoyed."

She laughed. "He does that every year. What is the third reason?"

Hollis adjusted his tie and straightened his shoulders. "Would you like to go out to dinner with me tomorrow night?"

8. IVY

OF COURSE, she said yes. A handsome, kind, employed man had asked her on a date. She wasn't an idiot. Even knowing Hollis wasn't going to be in town long, she'd still agreed to go. If the past year had taught her anything, it was that life was short and she should grab the good times as they came along.

Between arriving home at three in the morning, her anticipation of her upcoming date, and the to-do list she had running through her mind for the next day, she hadn't had the most restful night. Luckily, the Coffee Run was open every day. Marco, irritatingly looking like he'd had a full night's sleep, set her up with her daily dose of caffeine.

She and Maggie had cleaned up after the party, leaving the store ready for its annual Christmas decoration tsunami. The Teague women had a motto: let no surface go unadorned. Ivy had purchased her own ornaments and holiday accoutrements over the past couple years. When added to her mother's and grandmother's collections, she had three times more stuff than space.

Her first stop was the shop's storage room.

She needed to find the leftover vases and keepsake containers from the previous year. With any luck, her mom had squirreled some away, as well. However, luck was often disguised as hard work, and Ivy quickly realized she 'd have to empty the entire unit to get to the good stuff.

She didn't hesitate. She dragged every box and bag out of the storage room and heaped them under and around Captain's cage. "Are you ready to get to organizing, me hearty?"

"Arr."

Her hand hesitated above the first lid. "I wish Mom were here. This was her favorite time of year." Despite what people told her, the holidays did not get easier as time passed.

"Kisses!"

Ivy managed a little chuckle. "Thanks, Captain."

Her coffee had worn off by the time she finished separating the decorations from some half-full inventory boxes and her luck finally turned. With Elvis's Christmas carols being piped through the store, Ivy got to work, setting up an assembly line. She grabbed a green, pinecone-shaped bowl which had been popular two years earlier, hacked a piece of florist foam into a cylinder to make it fit, and then reached into the piles of flowers in front of her.

She hated to acknowledge Annie must be doing something right, but the other florist had been scooping up her customers at an ever-increasing rate. Ivy had swung by Love in Bloom on her way in and studied the holiday arrangements Annie had in her store window. Ivy wouldn't copy them, but she'd use them for inspiration without blinking.

She was so immersed in what she was doing, she jumped when she heard a rap on the front window. She looked up to see Hollis standing there. Brushing her hands on the apron she wore over her favorite, ratty, Canucks T-shirt, she bustled to the door. "Hollis? Is something wrong?"

"I was going to ask you that. Aren't you supposed to be closed on Sundays? How long have you been here?" He looked a little worse for wear. His scruff was a definite sign he was not on the job. It added a couple years to his face, dispelling the illusion he was fresh out of college. She liked it.

"I got here a couple hours ago. What do you think?" she asked him, stepping aside to give him a clear view. Ivy gestured at a trio of arrangements.

She had created precise, perfectly balanced, red-and-white centerpieces, then framed them with strategically hung garland and tinsel. She'd reallocated the wire-framed reindeer wrapped in white Christmas lights, which had traditionally stood by the cash register, and placed it in the corner of the window. The display looked flawless. And cold. She hated it.

"They're fine."

"Fine? What's wrong with them? The window looks like Love in Bloom's display," she said.

"That's what I mean. I've seen Annie's work. These are as conventional as hers. Don't be Annie. Be you," he said.

Hollis reached around her to pick up a huge tote filled with boxes of untouched Christmas ornaments. Ivy had popped the container's lid, but she hadn't bothered to dig any deeper after she realized it didn't contain any vases. The smaller boxes inside weren't a surprise; her grandmother had a special fondness for pre-loved, yard sale, Christmas ornaments. The ones on top of the box Hollis had grabbed were bright, mismatched, and every color and style under the sun. "Why didn't you use any of these?" he asked. "They have more real Christmas spirit than anything in the window."

"I didn't even know I had them until today. My grandmother bought holiday stuff like a squirrel collects nuts. I found oodles in the storage unit." Ivy would bet she had more tucked in the backs of closets and under the stairs at home. "It's a shame. These are antiques now. But nobody wants old-fashioned things like this nowadays."

She lifted a shoebox from the container and brushed off the dust. She removed the lid to reveal a stack of shapes cut from sheets of music with sparkles glued to the edges, and twig stars with their corners tied with silver thread. "It's too bad. These would make some awesome arrangements." They would be throwbacks to an earlier, less streamlined time, when homemade was valued more than trendiness.

Hollis reached for a small, flat box from the stack. "What's in this one?"

"I have no idea. Open it for me?" Ivy requested, still petting the glittery, paper bells.

He gasped. She did the same. A dozen, blown-glass candy canes lay nestled in tissue paper. Hollis held one up to the sunlight. The folded red-and-white stripes looked like ribbon candy with an ethereal glow. "I've been staring at Annie's decorations for two days. These are what ornaments are supposed to look like. Too bad you couldn't use them. They're exquisite."

"Who said I can't? They'd be perfect for a Christmas baby bouquet," she argued, noticing they'd switched sides of their argument. Ivy didn't have any emotional attachment to the decorations; she'd never seen them before. If she wasn't going to use them, they ought to go to people who would appreciate them. Plus, they would make a wonderful "Baby's first Christmas" keepsake. She was tempted to hold back one for herself, but business came first.

Ivy replaced the lid and tucked the box into the crook of her arm. "What else does she have in there?"

Hollis cracked open another bin. "Four mercury glass pickle ornaments. Why would somebody make a pickle as a Christmas ornament? I think it's a mistake. Should I toss them?"

"No! They're a thing in the U.S." Some family visiting from the United States would be delighted to receive a souvenir pickle in a centerpiece. The rest of the world may not know about the tradition, but they didn't need to as long as the flowers sold.

The entire tote was filled with ornaments that ran from antique to plain, old kitschy. Ivy could easily design arrangements around all of them—if she had the containers to put them in.

Then she opened four massive bins which had been pushed to the back of the storage room and hit the motherlode.

"Thank you, Grandma, for saving my bacon." Her eyes welled with tears that had nothing to do with the dust coating everything. One was crammed with candleholders, another with baskets. The third was a mix of candy and cookie jars, and the fourth contained ceramic holiday shapes like sleighs, snowflakes, and other wintery objects—dozens of them. She had more than enough to get her through the season.

The thickness of the dust indicated they must have been in the storage unit since her mother had moved Teague Flowers to Whistler decades before. Slowly accumulating junk must have pushed the tote boxes into the back corner, out of sight and out of mind. A few stretched back to the goofiness of the eighties, but Ivy remembered a lot of them from her childhood in the nineties, when the popular centerpieces were shorter and broader rather than the present day, tall-and-narrow style. They wouldn't be what everybody else was selling, but current styles weren't flying out of her store for her anyway.

No guts, no glory. If she was going to have to shutter her doors in the new year, she was going to go out on her own terms: fun, original, and overflowing with Christmas spirit.

"I don't understand. Isn't this stuff all too old to use?" Hollis asked. He held up a porcelain reindeer head, replete with antlers sticking out the sides like handles, and looked at her in confusion.

"I'd love new stuff, but I'm not going to get it. This is the next best thing."

"Why not? Can't you afford—Sorry, none of my business. Sorry."

She didn't mind the question—even if Hollis was playing her and taking all her dirty little secrets back to Annie. Although that didn't seem like something he'd do after being so helpful earlier. He couldn't make or break her business in the next week while he was in Whistler. It was all on her. Fortunately, she'd had great role models and refused to bow under the pressure. "Remember the call I got last night? And the paper I was holding? Someone cancelled my holiday vase order. It wasn't a data entry error. Somebody faked my letterhead and faxed a cancellation notice to my supplier. Maggie has been telling me my luck isn't truly this bad, but I can't imagine anyone being so underhanded."

"Couldn't you reorder the vases?"

"No chance. These boxes I found downstairs are literally going to save me, because the only new ones left to choose from are so generic they won't win me any points with customers. Now I don't have to pay for a huge order of holiday containers, which is money in my pocket. My grandmother may have just gotten me and the store through the Christmas season."

Hollis was oddly quiet. "Did you say a fax? Like, a paper fax?"

"Right? It's certainly one way to avoid leaving digital fingerprints. It was sent from the business center, so it could be anyone." Although she did have an idea. A vase in Love in Bloom's window looked surprisingly familiar. She'd already set a reminder for herself to call Brian back on Monday to see if he'd tell her if her entire order had been resold as one unit, or if it had been split up among several people.

Hollis looked thoughtful. "Will you have enough with your grandmother's boxes?"

"I will now. I'll order some plain stuff as backup, but this will give me an excellent start." If lightning struck and she went nuts with orders, she'd happily modify standard, red and green vases with Christmas bling from her craft stash. It was a problem she'd love to have.

"If my opinion makes a difference, I'd say go your own way. I've dealt with florists across the country. Love in Bloom fits right in with the big chains. If you want to do that, you'll always be up against stiff competition. If you deliberately choose to be original, the market will be wide open for you," Hollis said.

Ivy felt what her mom had called "her determined look" settle on her face. "You're right. I'm not Love in Bloom. Let them keep their fifteen-carnations-and-four-sprigs-of-spruce standard designs. I can do unique. My customers will each get a one-of-a-kind centerpiece, bouquet, or whatever they order. There must be a couple hundred ornaments here. I'm going for it." Her brain spun with possibilities. Maggie was going to have a fit. She'd been after Ivy to broaden her designs since she'd taken over the store. "I may not turn the same profit as Love in Bloom, but at least I'll enjoy coming to work every day."

"How about this? I'll finish decorating your window and the rest of the store, and you come up with some non-traditional arrangements to mix with the standard ones you've already made."

"Do you have any decorating experience?" She'd seen what her single, male friends called holiday decorations. Visions of garland hung unevenly along a shelf and a lopsided Christmas tree danced in her head.

Hollis looked genuinely insulted. "I'd wager I know more about Christmas decorating than you do. If you aren't impressed by the time I'm done, I will relinquish my personalized Santa hat, which is signed by Santa himself."

Ivy grinned. "That's a serious wager. What will I have to put up?"

"A second date."

"We haven't even had our first one yet."

"If you are that worried about it, I suggest you out-design me." He pushed up the sleeves of his sweater. "On your mark, get set, decorate!"

Ivy pulled together a red, blue, and purple blossom-filled explosion with shiny, twisty golden rods that screamed "holiday party." She made a long, low, cylindrical pot into the base for a lily and holly Yule log and turned a basket into a quiet woodlands-and-moonlight centerpiece for people who were looking for something less traditional.

But her masterpiece surprised even her. She filled one of the hideous reindeer heads Hollis had found with red, white, pink, and blue flowers and affixed a small pendant to a glass candy cane ornament so the year hung, clearly visible. There was no way any parent would throw it away. They'd remember the baby's Christmas bouquet every single year.

She placed her hands on her hips and arched her back. "That's it. I'm done."

"Great timing. Me, too."

"Nice job!" they said in unison as they took a minute to admire each other's work.

Hollis had aced it.

He'd used a quarter of the decorations she'd provided —maybe a third—and in her humble opinion, he'd transformed Teague Flowers into a vision that gave the winter wonderland outside a run for its money. He'd augmented the reindeer, turning it from a background character that blended into the four other shades of white in the window into a lively, colorful eye-catcher that pointed to the arrangements Ivy kept handing to him.

She'd seen him with the ladder but had been concentrating too hard on her own stuff to worry about what he'd been doing. Somehow, he'd hung ornaments and ribbons from the ceiling, creating the illusion of a floating Christmas tree in the corner of the room, which filled a blank space above her work counter. Instead of making any other large displays, he'd added touches of Christmas in unusual spaces. Customers would spy the decorations wherever they looked, but they were they were understated, which was going to work better than what she had originally planned.

"It's amazing. And now I have to send you away," she continued. Ivy took a deep breath. If she could be brave with flowers, she could do the same with Hollis. She wanted this date to go well. Really wanted it. She liked Hollis more by the minute, and it would be a waste if she didn't let him know it. She had some planning to do.

"What?"

"I acknowledge defeat. I need to go home and get cleaned up. I have to get ready for our dinner out. And I have a second-date outfit to organize."

"In that case, I will bid you adieu and meet you back here in two hours."

For the first time in months, she was happy to lose.

9. HOLLIS

HOLLIS COULD BE A GRACIOUS WINNER. When Ivy stepped around the corner two hours later, he became a grateful one, because any man who wasn't grateful for such an amazing, gorgeous date didn't deserve one.

She hadn't said anything about him moving the copy of the fax she'd been sent. He'd snapped a picture while he was putting away Christmas decoration bins. Maggie was right. Nobody's luck was that bad, and he had his suspicion as to where all her trouble was originating from.

"Where are we going?" she asked.

He couldn't believe how difficult that decision had been. Italian was usually popular but included the risk of splashing tomato sauce on his clothes. Sushi generally required chopsticks, and he wasn't proficient. He'd thought about asking Joel, but the Coffee Run had disappeared by the time he'd come up with that idea.

In the end, he'd decided to play it safe and wore a red shirt. "I hope you like Italian."

"Love it."

The breeze from earlier in the day had died, leaving a

beautiful, still evening. They dodged tourists scampering back to their hotels with ski bags swinging from their shoulders.

Ivy twirled spaghetti like a pro. "I love pasta," she said before she popped a forkful into her mouth. They had already demolished the bread basket and their respective salads. Decorating and flower arranging took more energy than Hollis realized.

"I never asked... Do you ski? You live here. I know Maggie skis. Joel and Marco snowboard. What about you?"

"I can ski. I generally don't," she told him. "I'll snowboard on occasion. How about you? Are you going to hit the slopes while you're here?"

"I'm pretty sure you got this when you asked me about the gondola, but I'm not a big fan of heights."

"You're not even going to try the bunny hill? It's a towrope. Your feet never leave the ground."

Hollis laughed. "Nope, not even that."

"What do you do for fun?"

He got her giggling at his fantasy team baseball league stories, especially when he described Nick's reaction the first time the victory monkey video had appeared on his computer. "Plus, I play real baseball in the summer—softball, really. It's our slow time at work."

They spent the rest of their meal and their walk back to the parking lot behind the store taking turns with funny stories. Hollis walked as slowly as he could to drag out their time together. He'd even talked Ivy into stopping for an ice cream cone. But at the end of the night, he had to say good-bye.

"Will I see you at the Coffee Run tomorrow?" she asked.

"You should. I'm here until I'm done at Love in Bloom. I can't see me finishing up before the weekend." If he did, he'd happily reimburse the company for a couple more nights at the hotel. They were expecting him back in the office on Monday. Between now and then, he could be where he wanted. He knew where that was. Maybe Ivy would get him on the bunny slopes after all.

He debated kissing her goodnight. He hoped to have another chance, so instead, he simply told her to have a good night and that he'd see her in the morning. Then she was gone.

Hollis replayed their dinner in his mind as he started walking back to the hotel. He was almost at the front entrance when he pulled his hands out of his pockets and realized his right one was bare. Since he knew he'd had both gloves when he'd held Ivy's hand as they walked to her car, he assumed he must have lost it afterward. He backtracked until he was two doors down from Teague Flowers but still hadn't spotted it. It had to be close.

He didn't expect to find a white delivery van idling behind the flower shop, especially not one with a Love in Bloom logo plastered on the side panel.

He recognized Justin Sprouse, Annie's toque-wearing delivery man. Before he could ask what Justin was doing, the part-time driver threw open the van's door and hopped out holding a loosely sealed cardboard box wrapped in a plastic tarp. He set the box under Teague Flower's fresh air intake duct, removed the wrap, and then bolted back into the van. Hollis flinched at the screech of spinning tires that left rubber on the road.

A mysterious package left for Ivy by her number one competition? He should probably call the bomb squad— or at least Ivy.

Hollis approached the package carefully. There weren't any labels on it. He got close enough to hear the box wasn't ticking. It was, however, buzzing.

He watched in dawning horror as a red-and-black insect crawled through the cracks in the folded-over flaps, flitted to the wall, and began moving to the source of the moist air blowing on it. The invader was quickly followed by half a dozen others.

A lady bug bomb. Not a technical term, but Hollis recognized it for what it was. Teague Flowers was about to be infested with a swarm of ladybugs. They didn't bite or pass along West Nile, but they got into every nook and cranny and were very expensive to get rid of.

Hollis had two options. Call Ivy back to the shop, where she'd have to call the cops and report the harassment.

Or he could return the box to the person who sent it. Technically, arguably, he could say that he saw the Love in Bloom delivery van drop it off. Hollis could claim he was returning it back to its rightful owners.

He didn't need to disturb Ivy. She'd had a couple of busy days. Plus, he didn't want the memory of their date scarred by this minor inconvenience. He'd do the friendly, helpful thing and return the box himself. When he picked up it up, he found his glove beneath it. Hollis considered it a sign he was doing the right thing.

He didn't leave it directly under the vent at Love in Bloom. That would have been wrong.

He gave it at least twelve inches. Maybe thirteen.

10. HOLLIS

HOLLIS DID NOT ARRIVE to his customary cup of complimentary coffee and warm croissant sitting on his desk. It took Annie ten minutes to realize he'd arrived at all.

"I don't have time to help you today, Hollis. We've been bugged. They're everywhere. I may have to close the store!" Annie was frantically running around with a fly swatter. Every surface was covered in moving red-and-black dots. "Have you seen Justin?"

"Not since yesterday," he replied honestly.

"I need to see him immediately. He made a terrible mistake."

Hollis didn't have time to correct her. He needed to review her papers. Well, one specific paper. Ivy's story the night before had reminded him of something, and he wanted to check if he was remembering things correctly.

"Justin, get in here!" Annie yelled as soon as her hapless delivery man arrived. She closed the door behind him, and the shouting started immediately.

Hollis dug faster. He found it at the bottom of the

pile: a receipt from the Whistler Business Center. It didn't indicate the number faxed, but the time stamp was dated two weeks earlier.

"I said it wasn't my fault," Justin yelled as he stormed out of Annie's office. "I put it exactly where you told me to, under the vent grill. It was a stupid plan anyway. And you can't fire me. I quit!" He pulled his toque down low over his forehead and stomped out the door without a backward glance.

Annie slapped the swatter on his desk, crunching three of the bugs near his calculator. "Hollis, I need to ask you to leave while I get this under control. I'm going to lose a whole day to this mess. It's all Ivy Teague's fault."

"Like the reviews?" Not that he had any doubt Ivy was innocent of any charges Annie threw at her.

"Exactly."

"I wouldn't make those accusations. I know for a fact Ivy had dinner out last night with people who can verify her whereabouts all evening. If you like, North Pole Unlimited can start an investigation to find out where the bugs came from. We can't afford for any of our affiliates to be involved in vandalism." Hollis chose his words carefully while keeping them all true. If someone were targeting one of their partners, they'd do everything they could to help. On the other hand, if a partner were a bad apple in the barrel—to paraphrase Adelaide—they had to be dealt with just as harshly.

"That's not necessary." Annie walked to the storage closet in the corner of the room and pulled out two cans of bug spray. "I won't say anything. But it is her fault."

She was partially right. Ivy had gotten vengeance without raising a finger. "I have an errand to run. I'll let you deal with..." He waved his hand around the room, swatting two ladybugs circling his head at the same time.

His first stop was at the Whistler Business Center. The owner remembered Annie; it was hard not to since he'd had to find the fax machine instruction book since neither of they knew how to use it. The machine's memory held the last thirty numbers dialed. Imprint Glassworks was the most recent number called. Hollis printed out the memory, paid for the page, and moved on to his next stop.

11. IVY

WHEN IVY ARRIVED in the village on Monday morning, life was fine. Beyond fine. The sun shone brightly without blinding her with its glare. A pair of brand-new, high-end mom mobiles in matching shades of metallic gray were parked one stall apart in her lot of choice, leaving her a spot conveniently close to the Coffee Run. Their owners were nowhere to be seen until three women with matching purses burst out of Love in Bloom, flapping their hands around their heads, screaming, and cursing.

Maggie, already waiting at the food truck, looked at Ivy in confusion as she fished in her purse for her wallet. "That's not a normal Love in Bloom customer reaction," Maggie said.

"I've got to know what happened in there. Go on, I'll catch up."

Ivy waited for the women to cross the street. She had no idea what they were after, but she was ninety-nine percent certain it had something to do with flowers. She could do that. And offer them a discount if they added a poinsettia to the order. Hollis's advice was slowly but surely making a dent in her surplus stock. If she had to drag customers off the street into the shop to get rid of the rest of them, she would.

"Are you okay? Can I help you with anything?" she asked as they approached.

"Get them off!" the leader said as she slapped herself in the head.

"Get what off?" Ivy asked.

"The bugs! I can feel them crawling on me!"

Ivy didn't see anything at first glance. Then she spotted a red dot moving on the woman's shoulder. Ivy brushed the insect away and grabbed the woman's flying hands. "That's it. They're all gone," Ivy told her.

"Are you sure?"

She stood still to give Ivy a chance to work. Ivy flicked a stray bug off the woman's purse strap, then said, "I'm sure. You're good." She performed the same service on the other two blondes, who finally calmed down. It was the first time she'd gotten a clear look at the invaders. How on earth had they ended up covered in ladybugs in December? "What happened?" Ivy asked.

"We went to Love in Bloom to order our holiday thank-you gifts for our volunteers, but the store was overrun with bugs. Absolutely crawling with them."

"That's horrible." Ivy managed to say it without laughing. The lights in her shop sprang to life at the other end of the village. "I don't know what you're looking for, but I have a flower store, as well." She pointed down the sidewalk to where Hollis's multi-colored reindeer lit up the window. "Among other things, we're having a sale on poinsettias if you need party decorations. Twenty percent off if you order five or more. Or, if you prefer a more individual approach, we have a guaranteed unique line at Teague Flowers. Although we offer traditional arrangements, you don't have to get the same centerpieces you see at Love in Bloom or any of the chain florists."

She was only halfway through her spiel when the leader grabbed her by the elbow and propelled her toward the shop. "We're desperate. Show us."

Ivy thought her new arrangements would speak for themselves once people got a look at them. She hadn't expected them to cause a pile-up in front of her window as people stopped to gawk, causing approaching pedestrians to crash into them.

"This one! I need this one," the short blonde in the group begged, jabbing at the Yule log behind the glass. "My mother-in-law is an absolute witch. This is so classy she won't be able to complain about it."

Ivy held the door for the women as they entered her shop. "I can do that for you."

They left with more than the Yule log. Ivy received an order for twenty poinsettias to be delivered to their art museum volunteer luncheon at the end of the week in the Villa Montague's ballroom. The women must have jumped on their cells as soon as they'd gotten into their vehicles, because the store phone rang off the hook with orders and inquiries about their hours and website for the rest of the day.

"Maggie, come here. You have to see this." An exterminator's truck had pulled up to the curb. They watched a pair of men with biohazard symbols on their overalls check a map. "I heard them asking for directions to Love in Bloom. That can't be good."

"It's very good. For us. Do you have any idea how much business we've done today?" her assistant asked.

"Enough to get us through the month if it keeps up."

"Better than that. I called Terkelson's down in Vancouver. Before you say anything—yes, it was necessary. I know you like to run lean, but after today, we will need a restock by midweek. I didn't go nuts. We might need another one later this week, too," Maggie said.

"Seriously?" Ivy couldn't remember the last time they'd needed an emergency resupply order, let alone two.

"Seriously."

They hustled all morning and through lunch to catch up on the surprising influx of orders, but they managed to stay on top of the wave. The sun was setting, and the cooler was stocked with deliveries for the next day, when the bell over the door sounded again.

"Happy Monday, Hollis," Ivy called.

"Is it?"

"It most certainly is. I have had the most amazing day." She was still riding the high of selling two dozen poinsettias in one day. They were a quarter gone now. Ivy was ecstatic.

"Tell me," he said.

Ivy didn't hide her glee as she regaled him with the events of the day, down to the hand-flapping by the women who had escaped Love in Bloom's infestation and the sales that had followed.

He beamed through her entire recitation. "Didn't I tell you that you had to make people think they were getting a deal? Congratulations."

"Thanks. The poinsettias are going to Villa Montague at the end of the week." Ivy told him.

"Wasn't that—"

"The place that cancelled their massive order at the

last minute and went with Love in Bloom instead? Yes. But those were for guests. These gorgeous, healthy, insect-free plants are for art museum volunteers. When you go back to the hotel tonight, if you happen to see a white-haired woman in a suit who looks like she French-kissed a lemon, be sure to wish her a good night from Teague Flowers."

"I'm sure Ellen will be thrilled," he said with a short laugh. "I'm sorry I'll miss it."

That didn't make sense. He stayed at the Villa Montague, and he'd specifically told her the manager never failed to find him to ensure the North Pole Unlimited representative was having a good stay. "What do you mean?"

"I'm headed out this afternoon. My work with Love in Bloom is almost over."

That's when she noticed he was fully loaded down. A briefcase hung from his shoulder on a thick leather strap, and he'd left a suitcase at the door. "What?"

"I filed my preliminary report last night. I have one final consultation with Annie this afternoon, and my boss wants me home tomorrow. I'm driving back to Vancouver today so I can fly out first thing in the morning."

"But..." He was supposed to ask her out again. Or, at least, give her a chance to ask him out. She knew they weren't going to have long together, but they should at least have a chance to say good-bye properly. Not end things like they were vague business acquaintances. Hollis stuffed his gloves in his pocket.

If he offered to shake her hand, she was going to deck him.

"I'm glad I got the chance to know you, Ivy."

Got to know me?

"I really enjoyed our time together," Hollis said.

Yes, that afternoon they'd spent playing bridge down at the retirement home would forever be burned into her brain. *Time together?* What was he talking about? It was like he was trying to pretend they hadn't dated at all.

"I wish we had longer," he continued, his voice even and cool.

He cut off suddenly. Ivy stopped staring at him in shock and started actually looking at him. His hands were still jammed in his pockets, and his jaw was clenched tight.

"Hollis?"

He shook his head, then slowly raised it till his hazel eyes met hers. "I'll never forget Whistler. Or you." He pressed his lips together again.

"You don't think you'll be back again. Won't you have to follow up with Annie?" she asked. She'd take anything. "You never even made it to the bunny hill."

"No." There was nothing left to add. He was trying to make a clean break of it, and Ivy understood why. She just didn't want to. It would have been smarter to have said good-bye after the biscotti incident, but she couldn't bring herself to regret their time together.

"Will you send me a text to let me know how your poinsettia sales go?" he asked.

"Sure." Ivy wanted to say something like, "We'll always have soup", or "I'll never forget our decorating competition", but Hollis was already at the door. "Have a safe trip. You're a good man, Hollis."

Then he was gone.

12. HOLLIS

HE WAS in no mood to be kept waiting, not after his horrible good-bye with Ivy. Annie may have been the reason he'd met Ivy, but she was also he had to leave her. It did not put him in a friendly frame of mind. "Great," Hollis said. "You're finished. We can wrap up the audit now." Then he could get out of Whistler and away from Ivy before he did something crazy, like put in for an unannounced vacation so he could learn how to ski. That would only make it harder to leave later.

"This isn't a good time, Hollis. I'm having a bad day." Annie's outfit, which had been pristine earlier first thing that morning, was rumpled and smeared with dirt.

"I can see that." He swatted at a ladybug that buzzed round his head. It was the only one he saw; Annie must have been successful in her eradication attempt. "I'm about to make it worse." Hollis set the fax receipt square in the middle of her desk. "Forging letterhead and signatures is fraud." He didn't know what the criminal penalty would be, but he was certain Ivy could hire lawyers who would.

Annie's red cheeks paled. "I have no idea what you're talking about. I didn't fax Imprint Glassworks."

"Stop, Annie. The good folks at the Whistler Business Center gave me access to their machine. You were the only person who has sent a fax in over a month. And you just confirmed it was you. I showed you a phone number. If you didn't fax them, how did you know was Imprint Glassworks?"

She snapped her mouth shut. He waited a minute for her to come up with an excuse. "I'm allowed to use a new distributor. I'm a florist."

Hollis nodded. "You are. I wonder, though... If I asked, would they tell me your order matched the one Ivy cancelled, down to the very last vase? Would the requests be identical, Annie?"

She didn't respond.

"I think you somehow got a copy of Ivy's order. I think you forged the letter and got Ivy's Christmas vase shipment cancelled before buying it yourself. I know for a fact you had Justin drop a box under Teague Flowers' ventilation duct." He held up a hand to ward off her interruption. "I was there. He didn't screw up, by the way. I saw him deliver it. You had no reason to deliver anything to Ivy after hours, so I returned it here. Not to mention, I heard him tell you he did it before he quit this morning." A bug landed on his nose, and Hollis went cross-eyed looking at it. "Obviously, if it had been something innocent, you wouldn't be dealing with a ladybug infestation at the moment. You planned a malicious attack on your competition, and it backfired. Now you have to deal with the consequences."

"What are you going to do? Technically, I didn't do anything to her. Teague Flowers is fine."

She was right, but the intent was enough. He had no proof she was behind the graffiti and vandalism, but with her history, he wouldn't doubt it. He didn't need to know about that; he already had enough to take action. Hollis was completely confident Adelaide Klassen and the rest of the company would back his next move, so he continued. "You purchased this store from Mr. Iverson a year ago, correct?" He already knew he had his facts right.

"Yes."

"Part of the purchase arrangement was taking on his existing contracts."

"Yes."

"Including the affiliation with North Pole Unlimited."

"Of course."

"Did you read the contract?" Hollis knew the answer to that question, too. Annie hadn't. If she had, she would have realized there was an entire section on corporate ethics and what affiliates could and could not do when it came to business practices. He didn't even feel bad. Before John had gotten sick, he'd called to ask if Love in Bloom needed help and had referenced the contract. Yes, North Pole Unlimited took a hard line, but they also agreed to provide support under the same section to keep things fair. Annie had blown two chances.

"No."

"You should have. You can consider this audit complete. Our head office will notify you of the results." He could have started proceedings immediately himself, but he didn't want the headache. Hollis just wanted the job done.

"But I'm making you money!"

"Money isn't everything." That was the company

policy, but Hollis hadn't realized how true it was until he'd met Ivy. He tried to be grateful for their few days together, but he was greedy. Like Annie, he wanted more.

He had to leave town before he did something drastic.

13. HOLLIS

North Pole Unlimited Headquarters
December, Manitoba

The poinsettia was a stupid idea. Its white petals reminded Hollis of the snow in Whistler, not like the stuff in Manitoba looked any different. And the red foil around the pot was exactly the same shade as Ivy's coat. The plant itself wasn't as nice as the ones at Teague Flowers, either; there was something about Ivy's poinsettias that made them feel more like Christmas.

He was an idiot. Hollis knew this. His plant was perfectly fine and probably a better quality than ninety percent of them out there, being as he'd purchased it from NPU's local supplier. But it wasn't one of Ivy's.

He could get rid of it, but then he wouldn't have any reminders of Ivy at all, and that was unacceptable.

Hollis had been home for over a week, and he missed his BC florist like crazy. But there was nothing he could do about it. The paperwork to sever NPU's contract with Love in Bloom had only filled his first two days home. Annie had protested; he knew she would. But the bad review and complaint filed by Villa Montague was the final nail in her contract coffin. Miss Franks had complained of the poor quality of her poinsettias, most of which had died in the first week of December.

Not that he cared that the hotel manager was upset; she'd caused Ivy a lot of grief.

His thoughts of Ivy were interrupted by a knock on the door. "What?" Even if he hadn't been working, he didn't want to be disturbed. He had enough on his plate to keep him occupied if he wanted to be. He was neck-deep in property acquisition requests from across the country. NPU's sports equipment manufacturing plant in Hamilton wanted to expand in the new year, and every building they suggested required a serious overhaul. Weren't there any factories in southern Ontario that didn't need new roofs?

The dark-haired kid in the corridor grabbed a tube from his mail cart and threw it at Hollis without stepping foot through the door, then took off.

He checked his email again. After Hollis submitted his report on Love in Bloom, he made a recommendation regarding Teague Flowers. It would take time to work its way through the system and security checks, but it was possible he could be in a position to offer Ivy something in May. Ivy could hold on that long. He'd asked Joel to keep him updated on Ivy and her store, and the matchmaker was happy to text him every morning when she picked up her coffee. Joel's prediction—her new arrangements were taking the Whistler area by storm, and they were only going to get more popular as the season progressed. Hollis was happy for her. She deserved the success, and even if a contract was the only contact he had with her going forward, he was going to do it for her.

He shouldn't care so much. Ivy was there; he was here. She had been a lovely distraction for a week while he'd been stuck in the mountains on a terrible assignment, but they had nothing in common. She was a small business owner; he acquired small businesses for breakfast. She had a pirate bird; he'd recently adopted a sleepy, black kitten named Midnight from the new veterinary assistant in Animal Care. They'd would never work, and a long-distance relationship wouldn't be enough for him.

There was another knock on the door. This time, his glare didn't send the person running. "You're scaring the interns. It's hard enough getting them to spend a year in small-town Manitoba without subjecting them to the wrath of the Dash," Nick Klassen said. He ignored Hollis's glare and made himself at home in the chair opposite Hollis's desk.

"Sometimes this job sucks. They should get used to it," Hollis replied. "What do you want?"

"Courtesy call. My grandmother is not pleased with your report."

"What was wrong with it?" He'd done exactly what he was supposed to: investigated a company and ended the association because they were negatively impacting North Pole Unlimited's brand. He'd assumed he was fine, because the day after he'd filed it, Nick told him he was a shoe-in for senior manager now that John Tinder was officially on leave. Hollis should be happy. He'd been working toward the promotion for months.

"The report itself was fine. But now we've got a region with no representation in mid-December. So, guess who gets to go out to British Columbia and get a new contract signed before Christmas to make sure we aren't left with a lapse of service?"

"You're kidding me!" He hesitated, looking for an excuse. "I just got home. And the holidays are next week. Surely, we have somebody on retainer. Can't we courier it to our west coast lawyers and have them do it? What's with the personal touch?"

"The company president insists that it be you. And what she wants, she gets."

"But—"

"Sorry, buddy. It's part of the job as Senior Mergers and Acquisitions account manager for the west coast."

"What?"

"Oh, did I forget to mention? You got the promotion. If John is able to come back to work, he asked to be moved to a lateral position so he won't have to travel. Jenny has more seniority than you, and she wants to move back to southern Ontario to be closer to her family. Which leaves you, sir, as the nominee for the British Columbia senior manager position. Congrats. You're going to need ski lessons."

He'd need more than that. He had to find a house in Squamish—conveniently located halfway between Vancouver for work and Whistler for Ivy—and buy motion-sickness medication for driving along all the mountain roads for his commute. The steep, twisty mountain roads. His stomach flipped at the thought. Rather than be upset, he decided it might be smarter to buy stock in the drug company.

But first, he had to tell Ivy. He'd left like he had because he'd known he couldn't ask her to come with him. He'd applied for his now-new position knowing a move was part of the package, but he'd expected Ontario. Ending up near her was a best-case scenario he hadn't dared dream. "I can't deliver a new contract now. I have stuff to do. Organize movers, pack. Plus, it's the holidays. I'm in charge of the cranberry sauce this year at the company potluck."

"I'm not the one you have to argue with. That would be the big boss. You know where to find her if you're brave enough." Nick stood. "I've got to go. I've been ordered to the Animal Care wing."

"Ordered? I thought Dr. Farnsworth reports to you. Aren't you her supervisor?"

"Not according to Joy."

Hollis grabbed his phone to call up his favorite list app and started to plan a cross-country relocation. He'd only added five items to it when he was interrupted again.

"Okay, Grumpy, let's go." Jilly Lewis tilted two suit-cases to standing positions. They sat squarely in the middle of his doorway, blocking any attempt at escape. "This is the last airport shuttle into the city this week. Dan and I can't wait to get out of here, even if it is only for a four-day weekend," she said.

"Am I going somewhere?"

Her smile faltered. "Nick didn't tell you? You're headed back to the west coast to get some contracts signed. The legal team in Winnipeg is going to meet us at the airport with the paperwork since this was such a rush job."

"I'm leaving now? Nick literally left my office five minutes ago. He didn't say anything about going today. I thought the contract just had to be signed before Christmas."

"Yes, now. You have thirty minutes to go home, pack,

and be waiting at the apartment building doors for pick-up." Jilly stared at him for minute. "Move it. Sun and fun await—at least, for me. If you make me miss my flight, I will make you pay."

"Where are you off to?"

"Orlando. Dan and I are going to ride rollercoasters until we puke."

"That sounds like a terrific vacation." The *not* was unspoken, but she laughed at him all the way out the door.

The highway was terrible; traffic was worse. They slid into the departures lane in front of James Richardson International Airport with only minutes to check in. A legal assistant Hollis recognized slipped him a thick brown envelope just before he walked into the security check area.

Hollis pulled out the contracts he was supposed to deliver. "Are you kidding me!"

Behind him, Jilly snickered.

"Did you know?" he demanded.

"Everybody knows," she said.

"I filed my recommendations two days ago. That's not nearly enough time for a full background check, let alone the rest of it. How is this even possible?"

She laughed again. "The recommendation to investigate Teague Flowers went before the board the day after you called in your first report. How could we not? I mean, the woman got you up a stepladder in the mountains to clean her store windows. She was obviously a good person, somebody you trusted, and someone you respected. Adelaide didn't need more than that to get started."

He stopped walking. Ivy had got him onto a stepladder, and he hadn't thought twice about it.

Jilly continued. "Hollis, it was obvious you fell for Ivy the moment you met her. You're the only one who didn't know."

That wasn't true. He knew he'd been falling for Ivy since the moment he met her. He hadn't realized it had been obvious two thousand kilometers away. As for the contract... That was plain, well-intentioned deviousness on his boss's part. He'd never seen it coming. Ivy certainly wouldn't. But... "If Nick knew I was getting involved with an affiliate's rival, why did he leave me there so long?"

Jilly shrugged. "It wasn't compromising your assignment. In fact, you were working harder because of it. Besides, I told him it sounded like you were having a good time."

14. IVY

Whistler, British Columbia

"Eighteen dozen gone!" she crowed.

Maggie knew what she was talking about. It was ten days before Christmas, and Ivy only had twenty-four poinsettias left in her shop. Even if they didn't get sold, it was an acceptable number. It hadn't been easy; it had been a battle to get every single plant out the door. But Ivy didn't have any complaints. And when Ellen Franks had come to her looking for replacements for the flowers in her executive suites—she said she couldn't afford to replace the rest of them—Ivy had magnanimously sold her three dozen healthy plants without a single dirty look. At full cost.

It was just business.

"One more order, boss," Maggie called out, inter-rupting her mental gloat. "Rush job. A massive arrange-ment for some guy's girlfriend."

"An apology bouquet?"

"No. He said this was a congratulation present for his girlfriend, who got a promotion after working her tail off. He said he wanted to celebrate it with her. Sorry, Ivy, no "I was a jerk" surcharge on this one."

It was an unofficial store policy. She generally gave sympathy flowers a discount. Jerks made up the deficit. It came out even at the end of the day. "Did he give any preferences?"

"Chrysanthemums—baby ones, if possible—asters, lots of greenery, and some large gerberas for accents."

Ivy's head came up in surprise. She'd get to play with all her favorite flowers in one display. As an added bonus, it didn't sound like she had to make it Christmas themed. She loved her new Christmas designs, but a change would be a nice way to end the week.

It would also keep her from checking her phone to see if there were any messages from Hollis. He'd been okay about texting her, but it was more infrequent than she would have liked. He treated her like a buddy; even Joel had more interaction with him than she did, and Hollis hadn't taken Joel out for dinner.

She knew she had a false image of Hollis in her head. He'd come into her life when she'd needed a knight in shining armor more than she ever had before, and everything he'd done made him the perfect candidate to pin all her hopes to. Even if he had been working with Annie. He hadn't promised her anything beyond the two dates he'd given her.

The future she'd built with him was entirely in her head.

And yet, she wasn't completely devastated. Disappointed, yes. But if she couldn't have Hollis, maybe someday, she'd find another knight to make her forget the one she'd lost.

"Ivy, do you want to do this one, or should I?" her assistant asked.

Considering Maggie had one hand on her skis, Ivy took mercy on her assistant. "I'll do it. Get out of here. See you on Monday." They were both going to enjoy their day off to rest and recuperate before the final Christmas push.

"It's a full moon tonight. I should get at least one good run in. The customer said he'd be in to pick it up just before six."

Since she was using all her favorite flowers, Ivy decided the recipient deserved a little something extra. Congratulation bouquets were a lot of fun to make and didn't come up often. She started with a bone white, twisted vase she'd been saving for a special occasion, grabbing it from the back of the cupboard. It was the perfect complement to the flowers she wanted to use. The recipient was going to be one lucky girl.

She'd stuck it in the cooler and was doing a final sweep of the floor as the clock approached six. She was putting the broom and dustpan in the back when she heard Captain announce someone enter the store. "Kisses! Kisses!"

It wasn't the parrot's usual greeting. "I'll be right out," Ivy called.

She didn't waste time. As soon as her customer paid her, she was locking the door and going home for thirty-six hours of enforced nothingness. Her grandmother's stash of old holiday containers had lasted three weeks. Fortunately, Ivy had seen the writing on the wall and had ordered the least offensive replacements she could get from Imprint Glassworks. She, Maggie, and a couple other local artisans had spent a wine-filled Sunday afternoon turning plain baskets and vases into a collection of Christmas- and winter-themed containers that should have lasted her another month.

They'd done it again a weekend later. She couldn't keep her new designs in stock. The antique, retro, and straight-up kitschy pots and containers struck a chord with her customers. People wanted to be reminded of the good old days, even if they were only a decade ago.

Ivy heartily approved, although it meant she'd be haunting flea markets in the new year to find new, old stock to ensure she could do it again next Christmas.

"I'll wait."

She knew that voice. "Hollis?" She had to be hearing things. Hollis was in Manitoba, probably rolling around on the flat prairie landscape and breaking hearts all over the province. Had he really come back to see her?

"I'm here to pick up a congratulation arrangement."

The truth of the situation hit her. The only reason he'd been in town at all was to work with Annie. He must be signing a new North Pole Unlimited contract with her. Annie couldn't very well be surprised if she made her own celebratory bouquet.

She couldn't believe Hollis had put her in such an awkward position.

The price just doubled.

She slammed the vase down onto the counter. Bits of baby's breath fell off, bouncing off the black, fake quartz onto her clean floor. "I'm sure Annie will love it."

He handed over his credit card without a word.

Only once she'd completed the transaction did he speak again. "It looks beautiful."

It was hard to stay mad at such a sincere compliment.

"Thank you. I had some good blooms to work with. It turned out well."

"I'm glad you like it, too. Since it's for you."

"What?"

"Annie probably would like it, but it's not for her. It's for you. I asked Maggie what your favorite flowers were."

The little sneak. First, she was going to yell at her assistant, then she was going to add a little something extra to Maggie's Christmas bonus.

"Why are you congratulating me? Did I win the lottery?" She'd definitely won something by having Hollis back in town, but she didn't know why he was there or how long he'd be staying. He could break her heart again if she got her hopes up.

He pulled an envelope from his suitcase. "I am pleased to offer you an affiliate contract with North Pole Unlimited. We will need a florist in the area beginning in the new year. The terms, conditions, and contract are in here."

It was everything she'd wanted. A month ago. "Will I be working with you?"

"You will. Of course, I'll have to check on you pretty regularly to make sure everything is going smoothly. We'd need to have business lunches. Maybe suppers. Is that okay?" He took her hand and brushed his thumb across her knuckles. "I hope that's okay."

She'd already been burned by him; she wasn't anxious to do it again. But he was the one who'd taught her to be brave, starting with her job. It had worked for her once. She could try it in her personal life. Ivy took a deep breath. "It's not the best idea. I'm not certain I could have a business relationship with you—not without hoping it turns into something more." The temptation was great;

she wasn't going to deny it. But she didn't want to put herself in a situation where her business was at risk, in addition to her heart.

Hollis's jaw dropped. Then he smiled like she'd told the world's funniest joke. "Okay. I'll tell Head Office we have a personal relationship. Nick can manage you. He'll be grateful for an excuse to come skiing."

Ivy's head spun. Her luck wasn't that good—not until lately. Was Hollis really here, saying what she thought she'd heard? She thought he'd felt the sparks between them, too, but he'd never given her any indication he was looking for more. "What are you saying?"

"I got the promotion I told you about. You are looking at NPU's newest senior manager in Mergers and Acquisitions. While I knew relocation was part of the job, I thought I'd be heading to southern Ontario, but my boss, and my boss's boss, had other ideas. They assigned me to the west coast. I'm going to be moving here. I was hoping that you could help with that. Maybe help me find a place, something between here and Vancouver?"

"You don't want to be based in Vancouver?"

"Ivy." He took her hand and led her out from behind the counter, then pulled her close. "I want to be based close to you."

"Kisses!" Captain squawked.

They both looked up and, sure enough, Hollis had them under the mistletoe again. "I'm working on it, Captain."

"You're moving here?" Ivy still couldn't believe it. After the terrible year she'd had, the last month had more than made up for it.

"As soon as I can manage it. So, are you going to help me find a place?"

"Yes. Absolutely."

Hollis wrapped his arms around her waist and picked her up, spinning her until they were both dizzy. Then he set her down and kissed her until she was dizzy in a completely different way. The corners of her mouth turned up when he pulled away. He'd used a beard wax that smelled slightly of spruce. He was going to fit right in with the skiers, snowboarders, and mountain climbers.

"And go out to celebrate my promotion with me?"

"Yes, absolutely."

He kissed her again. Captain approved and kept demanding more "Kisses!"

"And to celebrate your new contract with North Pole Unlimited?"

She'd completely forgotten about the contract. Laughing, she slapped at Hollis's hands on her hips and returned to the counter. She slipped the paperwork out of the envelope and began to scan it quickly. "You are inviting me to sign on as an affiliate to North Pole Unlimited. That's..."

Huge. They wanted to use her as their primary floral distributor in the area, and she'd be the preferred contractor for other affiliated companies. All it would cost her was a small discount. And she'd receive the same discount from everyone else under the NPU corporate umbrella. It was the business stability she'd been longing for. If she got in with the bigger hotels, too—which was a possibility after Annie's meltdown after the Villa Montague disaster—Ivy would have to expand. Get more staff. She'd need to make a new business plan, but even the thought of all the work excited her.

This time, she kissed him. She put everything she was feeling into it—all her happiness at his return, all her thankfulness about giving her a chance to make her business the success she'd always dreamed of, because she knew the contract had to come from him, all her gratitude for him taking a job in the mountains so they could be together.

She didn't want him to regret it for a second.

"Can I take that as a yes, you're interested in the contract?" he asked. "My boss is anxious to have this done by the new year."

Ivy put her bouquet back in the cooler. She'd pick it up on her way home, after their celebratory dinner. She'd planned the arrangement better than she'd known. "I'll have my people contact your people. Over dinner. Tonight."

"I look forward to it. NPU's first order will be a never-ending supply of mistletoe. We'll have to ensure you are keeping up on quality control."

"I'd only have the best mistletoe for North Pole Unlimited's newest Senior Mergers and Acquisitions account manager. But I think spot checks might be necessary."

"Daily spot checks." Hollis kissed her again.

EPILOGUE

Christmas Eve
   North Pole Unlimited Headquarters
   December, Manitoba

"Hollis Dash, put that phone away. You can speak to your young lady later. This is a party."

Nick Klassen watched his grandmother try—and fail—to get Hollis to hang up on Ivy. "It's a business call, Adelaide," Hollis argued. "Maintaining relationships with our affiliated companies is my primary duty as Senior Account Manager. I'd hate to have you think I was shirking my responsibilities the first month on the job."

She sputtered, and Hollis didn't wait for her to form a reply. Instead, he waved good-bye and wandered off—in search of a quiet spot, Nick assumed—to continue planning his move. In the last week, Nick and Hollis had scoured real estate boards looking for a place for him to live north of Vancouver. If they didn't find something soon, Hollis could be living out of a hotel for a month.

"I think the joke is on us," his grandmother said. "Here we thought it would be hilarious to send Hollis to the mountains for an assignment, and now he gets to live within spitting distance of the best skiing in the country."

"As much as he likes Ivy, I don't think he's going to be hitting the slopes any time soon."

His grandmother sighed heavily—hard enough to make him look at her in concern. He kept forgetting she was a sprightly seventy-something-year-old. A gentle kick to the shin of the head of I.T. opened up a chair, and Nick helped Adelaide take a seat.

"Would you like a glass of water?"

She shook her head and leaned into the cushioned back rest. "I'd like the pages on the calendar to stop flipping by so quickly. We've had a lot of changes this past year, Nick. Have you noticed?"

He had and figured it must be harder for her. Two of her contemporaries had resigned, moving on to their well-earned retirements. His grandmother lived and breathed for the company, but she had to be thinking of retirement, as well. He knew she was grooming his cousin to replace her. "I have, Gran."

The fatigue disappeared from her shoulders, and a wicked grin crossed her face. "I thought you might have. First Decker. Now Hollis. I guess this means you're up next for finding a sweetheart."

"I'm too busy with work to think about that."

"We'll see."

***

Romance continues to bloom at North Pole Unlimited, when Jilly plays matchmaker for her boss in

December (NICK AND EVE) and for a friendly baker in Calgary, Alberta (RUDY AND KRIS). Get the next two sweet Christmas romances in the series now in **Collection 2,** out now!

RECIPE: NO-BAKE COCONUT CHRISTMAS TREES

½ cup butter or margarine*
2 cups icing (confectioner's) sugar
3 tbsp milk
3 cups shredded coconut (medium or long strand)
½ tsp vanilla or mint flavoring**
Green food coloring* **
4 oz white chocolate for melting (chopped up baking squares or wafers) * **

Melt butter or margarine in a large saucepan or microwave. Remove from heat if using stovetop. Add icing sugar and milk.

Mix in coconut and flavoring. Add enough food colouring to tint mixture green.

Roll into 1" balls. Pinch tops to make into cones.

Place in refrigerator, uncovered, for at least 4 hours – preferably overnight – to dry and firm.

Melt chocolate in saucepan or microwave. Dip tops of "trees" to give make them "snow covered".

Makes 3 dozen treats.

Elle's Notes from experience

* You can get fancy and make "white" trees, however the more yellow the butter or margarine, the less white your trees will be (I recommend a very pale butter if you want to try this.) They look great with brown chocolate topping (melted chocolate chips work fine.)

** If you want to go retro to the 80's, you can make pink Christmas trees (remember those?) Tint the coconut mixture pink with red food coloring, add cherry flavoring instead of mint, and dip in white or brown chocolate.

Fall a Million Times

A Million Love Notes

ROYAL OAK RANCH

The Cowboy and the Movie Star

The Cowboy and the Pastry Princess

The Cowboy and the Constable

RESORT ROMANCES

Cuban Moon

Mexican Sunsets

Dominican Stars

Mayan Midnights

Complete 4 book boxed set

HEARTMADE COLLECTION

Brunch

Mains & Sides

Holiday Table

ABOUT THE AUTHOR

Elle Rush is a sweet contemporary romance author from Winnipeg, Manitoba, Canada. When she's not travelling, she's hard at work writing books which are set all over the world. From Hollywood to the house next door, her heroes will make you sigh, and her heroines will make you laugh out loud.

Elle has a degree in Spanish and French, barely passed German, and is learning Italian and Filipino. She flunked poetry in every language she ever studied. She also has mild addictions to tea, yarn, terrible sci-fi movies, and home renovation shows.

To keep up with news and upcoming releases, sign up for her newsletter at **www.ellerush.com/news-letter** or follow her on Twitter (@elle_rush) or Facebook (Elle.Rush.Romance).

Manufactured by Amazon.ca
Bolton, ON

34079056R00120